The

The detonator timer ticked the seconds away: 15 ... 14 ... 13 ...

Marine Captain Halley summoned every ounce of strength he had left in his body. Without thought for his own safety, he hurled himself toward Metal Gear, his right hand reaching for the white button that would disarm the weapon.

But his hand never made it.

As Halley leapt through the air, with only seconds to spare before detonation, the dictator CaTaffy raised his pistol ... and fired.

METAL GEAR®

A novel based on the best-selling game
by ULTRAGAMES®

Book created by F.X. Nine
Written by Alexander Frost
A Seth Godin Production

**This book is not authorized, sponsored, or endorsed
by Nintendo Company Ltd.**

Hippo Books
Scholastic Publications Limited
London

This book is dedicated to my son, Alex.

Special thanks to: Greg Holch, Jean Feiwel, Dick Krinsley, Dona Smith, Amy Berkower, Sheila Callahan, Nancy Smith, Joan Giurdanella, Henry Morrison, Michael Cader, and especially Emil Heidkamp, Kay Wolf-Jones, and Kim Lee

Scholastic Publications Ltd,
10 Earlham Street, London WC2H 9RX, UK

Scholastic Inc.,
730 Broadway, New York, NY 10003, USA

Scholastic Canada Ltd,
123 Newkirk Road, Richmond Hill,
Ontario L4C 3GF, Canada

Ashton Scholastic Pty Ltd,
PO Box 579, Gosford, New South Wales,
Australia

Ashton Scholastic Pty Ltd,
165 Marua Road, Panmure, Auckland 6,
New Zealand

First published in the USA by Scholastic Inc., 1990
Published in the UK by Scholastic Publications Ltd, 1991

Copyright © 1990 by Seth Godin Productions, Inc.

Metal Gear® is a registered trademark of Ultra Software Corporation.
ULTRAGAMES® is a registered trademark of Ultra Software Corporation
WORLDS OF POWER™ is a trademark of Scholastic Inc.

ISBN 0 590 76482 9

CHAPTER ONE

The Mission

Justin Halley strode purposefully through the underground hallways of Fox Hound Command. At age twenty, he was the youngest captain ever to serve in the U.S. Marines Special Forces antiterrorist squad known as the Snake Men. His code name — Solid Snake.

Halley had a lot on his mind.

Three weeks earlier, fifteen Snake Men, half the squadron, had been dispatched from their underground training base on a top-secret mission. So far, not a single one of them had returned. Were they dead? Captured? Nobody knew. And none of the remaining Snake Men dared to speak of it out loud. They could only wait and wonder.

Now, of the fifteen Snake Men left, only Justin Halley had been sent for. The order had come directly from Commander South, head officer of Fox Hound Command, the military unit controlling the Snake Men.

As Halley entered the Command

Center, he saw that the vast room was empty except for three people — himself, Fox Hound Commander South, and South's brand-new second-in-command, Lieutenant General West.

As usual, Commander South was in combat fatigues, generals' stars on his shoulders, colorful campaign ribbons and medals pinned to his chest, his camouflage pants tucked into his high-laced boots. A battered old beret with the insignia of the Snake Men was pulled down at an angle on his head. The beret had been with Commander South all the way through his many paratroop missions in Vietnam, and he'd sooner part with his right hand than with that ancient piece of clothing.

Lieutenant General West was wearing his dress blue uniform, freshly cleaned and pressed, and so stiff that it could stand at attention all by itself. The spit polish on his black shoes gleamed. West was a by-the-book kind of officer, but he'd improve with time. The Snake Men squad would see to that.

"Solid Snake, we have a special mission for you," South told Halley, who stood straight and tall before him at attention, his dark blue eyes front. "But it's voluntary, Captain Halley. You don't have to go. It may very well cost you your life. In fact, the chances are ten thousand to one against you."

"Sir!" Justin called out snappily, his gaze never wavering.

"Have you ever heard of Doctor Ivan Pettovich?"

"Doctor Pettovich? The astrophysicist and nuclear scientist who defected to our side from the Soviet Union six years ago? Yes, sir."

"That's the man. Eight months ago he was kidnapped, and he seems to have disappeared off the face of the earth. We expected to hear that one terrorist group or another was claiming credit for his capture and was holding him hostage, but no word came. We didn't know if he was alive or dead.

"Now we believe that he is in fact alive, but a prisoner. For some months now, our intelligence forces have been picking up random clues. We thought, at first, those clues were unconnected. But when we put them all together over a period of time, they began to point to a strong possibility. Now we're fairly certain that Doctor Pettovich is alive and is hidden in a secret base of Colonel Vermon CaTaffy's, a base called Outer Heaven."

Halley's eyelids flickered, but he said nothing. No junior officer, not even one of the Snake Men, would dare to offer a comment to his commander unless asked to do so. But his pulse raced with excitement.

Colonel Vermon CaTaffy! The single most feared terrorist on the planet, a psychopath bent on dominating the world, his nature so cruel as to verge on insanity. He was a total paranoid, his deeds those of a madman.

Colonel CaTaffy was dictator for life of his small but incredibly wealthy and savage desert country, Nouria. CaTaffy's sole purpose in life was to bring the democratic nations to their knees. His terrorist actions were hideous, violent, always unexpected.

And always effective, because they struck fear into the hearts of world leaders. CaTaffy bombed civilian aircraft, killed innocent people, took non-combatants hostage, and tortured them without mercy.

A mission against CaTaffy! Halley felt his heart swell with eagerness. Also, here was a chance to rescue his buddies, the lost Snake Men!

Commander South continued, "We now believe we've located the secret base. Satellite reconnaissance of a distant jungle has revealed an unfamiliar complex of buildings, not in Nouria...but...somewhere else. I'm not authorized to share that information with you. It's got the highest possible secrecy classification.

"I can only tell you it's impossible to conceal a compound of that size and fortification in a desert country. So they went to the jungle instead.

"Computer scans of the satellite photographs show a huge base, larger than anything we've dealt with before, heavily protected, and made up of a number of buildings. Halley, it's our belief that this compound is Outer Heaven, and Doctor Pettovich is held prisoner somewhere in there.

"Two weeks ago, Doctor Pettovich's daughter, Ellen, disappeared. Witnesses tell us that she was snatched from her college campus as she was leaving her dorm. Three masked men carrying automatic weapons jumped out of a long black limo with phony license plates, forced her inside, and took off at eighty miles an hour.

"We believe now that Doctor Pettovich didn't give in under torture. Now we're afraid that top-secret nuclear information may have been taken from him, because they're holding his only daughter prisoner, threatening to torture or kill her.

"But that's not all...there's something

else, Halley. Something even more ter-rifying. Something that has us really worried.

"Our intelligence sources have hinted at something called Metal Gear. What Metal Gear is and when it's scheduled to be launched against us, we don't know. We don't know what it looks like, whether it's airborne, or how it's armed. We don't know how or even whether it can be dis-armed. We presume it's controlled by some hidden supercomputer, and that it carries a nuclear payload. But we can't be certain of any of this. Our information is too fragmented and too obscure.

"All we're sure of is that Metal Gear is the most powerful and evil weapon ever devised. It could destroy our planet and every living thing on it. We've got to stop it before it's too late. Stand easy, Solid Snake."

Justin Halley took a step to the side and locked his hands behind his back. All his attention was focused on Commander South's words.

"Three weeks ago, we parachuted half our Snake Men squad into the jungle, hoping they could infiltrate CaTaffy's hidden base and rescue Doctor Pettovich, or at least bring us back useful data on Outer Heaven and Metal Gear. Not a single one of them has come back. They may be all dead.

"There is some chance that one or more Snake Men may be held as prisoners. Our information on that is very scanty, I'm sorry to say. We can only hope that at least some of our men are still alive."

Halley's skin prickled in anger and revulsion at the thought of his friends ... good men, perhaps dead, or, even worse, alive and under torture. Yet he said nothing. No flicker of emotion showed on his face. Only the strong muscle in his jaw clenched tight.

"Understand me, Captain Halley. This will be your first solo mission, but there's a very good chance it may be your last one. Beyond doubt, it's a suicide mission. We want you to locate Outer Heaven, then search for and destroy Metal Gear."

Destroy Metal Gear? A solo mission against overwhelming odds? Justin Halley's neck hairs prickled at the idea of it, and the excitement made the red blood rush through his veins.

CHAPTER TWO

Mission Accepted

"We want you to go in alone," continued Commander South, "armed with nothing more than a compass. If you try to break in fully armed, you'll be slowed down. You won't last five minutes. We want you to be a shadow, to slip through unseen. Do you read me?"

"Yes, sir!" Every nerve in Halley's mind and body were on red alert.

"Whatever weapons or equipment you need, you'll have to find on the spot or make do without. Speed is what's important here. This mission has to be completed within hours of your arriving in Outer Heaven." Commander South's stern face and steady gaze told Solid Snake as much as his words did — that this mission was of the utmost importance.

"Look for a transceiver radio; when you locate it, tune it to Fox Hound Command's secret frequency. Then you'll be able to receive our radio transmissions.

"If you find any Snake Men alive and held as hostages, set them free. Rescue as many as you can, and we'll pick them up later.

"But be careful, very careful, Captain Halley, even when dealing with Snake Men. Don't take anybody's word or anything at face value. Some of the Snake Men may have broken under torture and turned double agent. You won't know for sure which of them you can trust.

"As for Ellen, Doctor Pettovich's daughter, we don't know whether she's alive or dead. If you find her alive, she may be of some help with her father. Try to rescue Doctor Pettovich, too, but if you can't, then you'll have to kill him. He's more valuable to the free world dead than alive and in the dangerous hands of Colonel CaTaffy. Understood?"

"Sir," said Solid Snake. It was understood. In the game of terrorism, the stakes were high . . . and often fatal.

"The compass you'll be carrying is the latest technology. It will transmit everything you say, and it contains a homing device. We'll be monitoring you constantly on the Command Center's computer screens.

"By means of the homing device in the compass, we'll be able to locate your position with pinpoint accuracy and target you to receive the radio transmissions that will give you all the up-to-date information we have. You won't be able to hear us through the compass, so you'll need to locate that transceiver as quickly as you can.

"As you penetrate the base, the radio broadcasts will help you as much as we can. You will be contacted by our agent, code named DIANA, on wavelength 12033. She will be your Control. She may sometimes identify herself as Boss Man. We can't tell you any more than that."

Once again, Captain Halley, only nodded without speaking. He understood fully the need for secrecy.

"Once you're in Outer Heaven, you're completely on your own," continued Commander South.

"We can't tell you how the base is fortified, or what traps Colonel CaTaffy and his forces might have set to detect your presence and kill you. You'll have to elude all their traps, deal with their security forces, find our lost Snake Men and Doctor Pettovich, locate which building houses Metal Gear, and somehow destroy the terrible weapon. It's a big job, Solid Snake, a very big job.

"It's the biggest mission one man has ever been sent on. Fifteen good Snake Men have already gone in and not a single one has come back. We can't afford to lose the rest of the squad. We're counting on you and you alone.

"But the decision has to be yours. We can't order you in there, to face almost certain death. Will you do it? Knowing the one chance in a million you have of coming out alive, do you still volunteer?"

"SIR! Yes, SIR!"

"Good. You'll leave in an hour," said Commander South, nodding. "We haven't a moment to spare. But first, get rid of that uniform you're wearing." South scowled at the crisp olive-drab fatigue suit that covered Solid Snake's muscular body.

"We don't want you wearing or carrying anything that links you to your unit. This mission is top secret. We're issuing you a special camouflage suit. Pick it up at the quartermaster's, put it on, and be back here at 1400 hours. No dog tags. Wear no identification of any kind. Take nothing else with you that might connect you to Fox Hound and the Snake Men with the exception of this compass. Is that clearly understood? Nothing."

"Yes, SIR!" Justin saluted snappily, turned on his heel, and marched out.

As the door to the Command Center closed behind Halley, Commander South sighed deeply and rubbed his hand over his brow.

"Do you think he bought it?" asked General West softly.

"Halley? He'll do as he's ordered; he's the best of the Snake Men. I hate to lose him. He's highly trained and qualified. It galls me to have to sacrifice Solid Snake, but that's the way it has to be if we're to stop this madman CaTaffy and his new infernal deadly weapon Metal Gear."

"Tell me about the Snake Men. Who are they?"

For a fraction of a second South hesitated. The information on the squad was highly classified, top secret, but West was his new second-in-command, and therefore entitled to be briefed.

"Code name Snake Men is a unit that doesn't 'officially' exist. You won't find them on any roster in the Pentagon. But somewhere in Utah in a silo deep underground, a picked elite force of thirty young Marine officers has been undergoing intensive antiterrorist training. It's a different kind of training from anything you've ever imagined, West."

"In what way?" General West asked curiously.

"In addition to being chosen for their courage, their intelligence and loyalty, for their incredible physical stamina and co-ordination, the Snake Men have been taught to survive with their bare hands.

"They've learned to create equipment and weapons out of nothing more than a hostile terrain, any kind of terrain from big city to deepest jungle to driest desert. At the same time, they've been getting top-secret training in twenty-first century weapons that the world believes are still only on the drawing boards. I'm proud to say that our Snake Men are trained to handle virtually anything.

"Most important of all, this unit has been selected for their intelligence and swiftness of mind. The Snake Men have been trained to use their brains, to out-think their opposition, to project themselves into the actual mind-sets of the enemy, so that they can strike first, just like the snake for which they're named.

"Snake Men use their brains before their guns in any situation, even when it threatens their own lives. Yet, they obey without thought or question the orders of a superior officer. In a world filled with warfare and terrorism, where space-age technology has made the destruction of the earth more than a possibility, the Snake Men have been chosen to be saviors."

"And Halley?

"As I said, Justin Halley is the best of the Snake Men. He'll be almost impossible to replace, but we have no choice. Metal Gear is the most serious threat to democracy we've ever been up against. It's a weapon of unlimited potential for destruction. The future of the free world depends on our finding it and destroying it."

"If you're going to use Solid Snake as a diversion device, then why did you give him the compass?" prompted West.

"It's a phony. It's just an ordinary government-issue compass, nothing special about it. It's just something for Halley to hang onto. But we will definitely be tracking him. The real homing device is a microscopic electronic unit sewed into the left sleeve of his new camouflage suit. That way JEN-NIFER can pinpoint him for radio transmission."

"JENNIFER? You told Halley DIANA would be transmitting over the radio."

Commander South chewed at his lip. "JENNIFER will also be transmitting, but Solid Snake won't actually pick up her signals because she'll be on a different frequency. He'll get DIANA's instead, and she'll lead him around with false clues for as long as possible, so that we can buy a little time to set up the real raid."

"So Halley is to be used as nothing more

than a decoy?" General West looked puzzled.

"I'm afraid so. We're sending him in to create a diversion, a smoke screen. Then the real attack by the full forces of Fox Hound Command can take Colonel CaTaffy by surprise, catch him off guard, defeat him, disarm Metal Gear, save as many of our Snake Men as are still alive, and rescue Doctor Pettovich and his daughter."

The Commander smiled very sadly, and West could see the pain in his eyes. It was obvious that Commander South hated the deception he'd been forced to practice on his Marine captain, Justin Halley. "Captain Halley — Solid Snake — is brave and loyal, and very fast on his feet. Most of all, he's logical and quick-thinking. Of all the Snake Men we have left he'll buy us the most time."

"So what you're is saying that Captain Halley is expendable?" asked West.

Commander South sighed hopelessly. "Worse than that . . . he's disposable."

CHAPTER THREE

Getting In

Justin Halley sat in the dark glider, his long legs cramped up almost to his chest, his seat belt buckled across his shoulder and lap, the parachute strapped to his back. He'd been sitting like this for many hours. The glider was completely sealed; his little cockpit let in no light.

Halley had no idea what direction the mother plane had carried him. All he knew for certain was that, at some predetermined point, just before the jet came within radar range of Outer Heaven, the glider had been released. Soon it would lose enough altitude to come in low and escape enemy radar detection. Later, at some other preset time, the explosive bolts of the glider's cockpit cover would release, and Halley would parachute out and down into the unknown. From there, he'd be on his own.

The sudden sound of the cockpit bolts exploding startled Halley. But the instant his eject seat hurled him out of the glider, every one of his senses was on red alert. The chute opened without effort, unfurled like a giant silken sail, and carried Solid Snake silently to earth.

He snapped the lines free and gathered the folds of the chute into a bundle he could carry. Now he looked around him, trying to see something — anything. But visibility was zero.

Halley had landed in complete darkness, in the middle of what felt like — and smelt like — jungle. Trees and vines were all around him, and there was a heavy, warm mist rising from the jungle floor. Seeing anything at all was impossible.

"Down and safe," he spoke into his compass, hoping that someone at Fox Hound Command was on-line and was monitoring him.

All around him, Halley heard the sounds of the jungle, of wild beasts, night stalkers, and killer animals. It was too dark to travel. He'd have to wait until dawn.

Climbing up into a nearby tree, Halley disturbed a sleeping tribe of little red monkeys, who scattered through the branches, angrily chattering. Justin wrapped the parachute around him and settled into the crotch of the tree, to grab a few hours of uneasy sleep. He didn't know when he'd get the chance to rest again.

Three hours later, Halley awoke. Although the sun could barely pass thro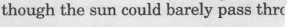

the thick jungle canopy, enough light penetrated to rouse Halley. All of his senses on red alert, he looked around him in every direction. Apart from the animal and bird sounds of early morning, there was nothing, Justin climbed down silently to the jungle floor and set out on his mission, the search for Outer Heaven.

Some highly developed instinct, the result of his Snake Man training, led his feet west. He noticed that there were fewer birds and monkeys in that direction, and fewer animals always spells the dangerous presence of man. Animals were far from stupid. They could teach man a few tricks about survival in hostile terrain. So west Halley went, keeping low and as quiet as possible.

As he moved without sound through the jungle, Justin Halley found himself suddenly in a patch of jungle growth that was fouled by a strong, almost sickening odor.

His nose wrinkled. Solid Snake recognized that smell — panther musk. It might be a useful weapon.

Rubbing himself against the jungle plants, Halley let the heavy, musky cat smell seep into his suit of "camos." Now he smelled exactly like a jungle killer. Other animals would keep out of his way, unless of course he should bump into another male panther. Then he'd be in for the battle of his life.

Solid Snake smiled at the thought of himself in a cat fight, although it would be no laughing matter if it actually happened.

At last, after three more miles of trudging through dense dank vegetation, Justin Halley saw light ahead. That could only mean a clearing, a man-made clearing. Trees had been cut down around a huge circle, several miles wide, and the leafy canopy had a large hole in it now. Sunlight poured down.

Careful, now. Halley crouched down and edged forward very slowly. On the edge of the clearing he stopped. Bingo.

Three military trucks, with a strange insignia painted on their sides, were parked in the clearing, two of them close together, and the third one much further off. The insignia — a grinning, fanged reptile entwined around a twisted broken tree — was something Halley didn't recognize, but it had a menacing quality that struck a familiar chord deep inside him.

It told him that Metal Gear wasn't far away.

Beyond the trucks, about half a mile away and surrounded by a high electrified fence, stood a vast compound of sealed off buildings. They appeared to be made of cast concrete or heavy stone, and they had no visible windows.

Solid Snake grinned. The satellite photos of Fox Hound Command were on target. This massive and menacing compound must be Outer Heaven. Solid Snake sat back and spoke softly into his compass.

"I think I'm at mission site. I have visual ID of potential target. Looks like Outer Heaven, guys."

He waited a minute, hoping for a reply, maybe a beep of some kind to let him know that his home base had him on the computer screen, but there was no return transmission.

Was the monitoring system working, or had he been cut off from Fox Hound Command? He'd have to locate a radio transceiver as soon as possible to find out.

Justin stood up carefully, looking in every direction. As he did, the jungle silence was broken by a sudden ear-splitting chorus of snarls and growls. Six barking killer dogs, giant half-starved Dobermans, burst out of one of the trucks. Their fangs were enormous, white and sharp; their powerful jaws dripped foamy saliva. Snapping and howling, they raced toward Halley at top speed.

CHAPTER FOUR

Inside the Gates

In his training with the Snake Men squad, Justin had learned an entire language of commands to control killer dogs. He could get them to "halt" and to "sit" in German, Russian, Swahili, Chinese, Japanese, Arabic, and a dozen other tongues. But he had no idea in what country he was now, not even which continent. His canine vocabulary would be of no use here. He had only seconds to spare.

No way could Solid Snake outrun this pack of trained attack dogs. Without a weapon, he couldn't even defend himself. Even if he managed to snatch up a branch from the jungle floor and use it as a club, Halley was no match for half-a-dozen frenzied attack dogs who lived only to tear out an intruder's throat.

Suddenly, an idea struck him. It was a crazy idea, but it could be his only chance!

Throwing himself to the ground, Halley raised himself on all fours, like a giant cat, bracing himself as the dogs came clo

He could smell their hot, strong breath and see their insane rolling eyes. Most of all, there were those sharp white fangs, less than a foot from his face!

Now the killer dogs had almost reached him. They were only inches away from chewing him into raw hunks of bloody flesh. Solid Snake arched his back high. He snarled and growled, low in his throat, meanwhile staring hard at the lead dog with narrowed angry eyes. Drawing his upper lip back, Halley spat and yowled like a furious giant cat.

Just as they heard Halley's unearthly sounds, the strong scent of the panther musk on his camouflage suit hit the dogs' sensitive noses.

Jungle predator! A male panther! Between the sounds and the smell, the Dobermans perceived Solid Snake as a big cat. One hundred seventy pounds of pure panther power, with incredibly strong teeth and claws sharp enough to rip a dog into confetti. The Dobermans skidded to a halt, yelping, then turned tail and rushed away, almost knocking each other over in their eagerness to escape.

Laughing under his breath, Justin Halley watched them go. Then Halley's expression turned serious. He had some heavy work to do. Crouching low, he slipped silently, almost invisibly, across the clearing to the nearest truck, about fifty yards away. He kept his eyes peeled for guards, but saw none.

Empty. The truck stood empty. No guards — no dogs. On the seat in the truck's cab, a pair of powerful rubber-cased field binoculars had been left. Solid Snake's hands closed around them in triumph. The binoculars were the first piece of the equipment he'd need. Now he was on his way.

Should he commandeer this truck? No, the third truck, parked furthest from him, was closest to the gate of Outer Heaven. That was the most useful one. By the time he'd made his way over there, he'd know if any of the trucks were guarded.

The second truck was, in fact, guarded. Inside the cab, the uniformed guard, a muscular man with a heavy black mustache, was drowsing in the front seat.

Halley came up behind him without a sound; the man only turned in his sleep, snoring.

Two swift rabbit punches from Solid Snake's strong, quick fist and the sleeping guard was out like a light, on a one-way ticket to Dreamland. One down. But was the sleeping guard alone? Guards almost always come in pairs.

A sudden noise behind him made Halley turn. Another uniformed guard, tall and heavy, was leveling an automatic weapon at Solid Snake's stomach, growling something in a guttural language Halley didn't understand. But Justin could see the guard's finger tightening on the trigger.

Lightning fast, Halley aimed a knee kick and connected. With a cry of pain, the big man went down, and an open-handed chop to his hairy neck finished him off for now. He lay still, not even twitching.

Solid Snake looked around. The overpowering of the two guards had been so swift and silent that no alarm has been raised. Yet. But it could happen at any moment.

Should he take the guard's Kalashnikov automatic weapon? No, Halley might encounter metal detectors on his way into the Outer Heaven compound. Better wait until I'm inside, he thought.

But something else caught Justin Halley's eye. He knelt down at the side of the fallen guard.

Attached to the big man's uniform by a pin was a plastic card, bearing that same strange insignia and encoded with a series of raised symbols. Halley recognized it immediately as a key card that might activate at least one of the electronic doors and gates of the Metal Gear base.

The fallen man must be an officer, to be authorized to carry a key. This was a real piece of luck. Solid Snake pocketed the key card and moved rapidly toward the third truck.

The third truck was empty and unguarded. It was parked fairly close to the gate of the base. Justin Halley got behind the wheel and put the truck into low gear. The vehicle moved slowly toward the entrance of the base. Driving with one hand and feeling around on the front seat with the other, Solid Snake found a package of half-eaten rations.

Evidently the men must have recently had their breakfast. Cautiously, he took a nibble, tasted it, and made a face. Government-issue field rations are the same all over the world, he thought. They may be packed densely with nutrition and vitamins, but they taste like a cross between cat food and an old rubber tire. Even so, he chewed the rations quickly and swallowed grimly. No telling when he'd get another meal, and this so-called "food" would at least give him a quick energy boost.

Also on the seat was a pack of cigarettes. Halley reached for them, but drew his hand back. Could they be poisoned? His insti told him that they could be a deadly trap. And, even if the cigarettes contained no added poisons, they were deadly enough in themselves. He decided to leave them where they were. But he did take the matches; matches could be used in many ways.

The truck was at the gate now. Solid Snake slipped out of the driver's seat and crouched down, keeping the vehicle between him and the gate, while his quick eyes darted around, checking for guards.

Two armed men were patrolling, but they were overconfident, talking to each other in that same strange language. They didn't expect to see Halley, so they didn't see Halley. He had made himself into a shadow, as he'd been trained.

Holding his breath, Solid Snake waited until they passed along to the far side of the electrified fence.

Then Halley duck-walked up to the gate, looking for the electronic lock. When he reached it, he stood up. This was it.

Would the key card in his hand be the one that opened this locked gate? Or would the alarm go off, bringing guards running from all sides? Only one way to find out. Halley pressed the embossed side of the card against the lock. For a split second, nothing happened. Then . . . a click.

The gate opened, and Halley ran inside,

swifter than a shadow and just as invisible.

"I don't know if you're copying, but I'm in," he whispered into the homing device, the compass he'd been carrying. No radio, so no response.

Once again, Justin wondered if anyone back at Command could hear him. Maybe the compass was defective. Maybe the transmission channel was blocked or scrambled. Maybe....who knew? The possibilities for a mess-up were almost endless.

What he didn't know was that although the compass was really just a compass, he was transmitting after all, through a hidden microradio that had been sewn into his sleeve back at the base.

"He's in," Commander South announced, his eyes on the large computer screen.

"Heaven help him," whispered General West.

CHAPTER FIVE

Level One

Hiding in the shadow of one of the empty trucks parked inside the compound, Solid Snake took a long look around.

What Halley was looking for was something that would give him an indication of where Metal Gear might be concealed. A hatch leading to an underground silo, maybe. Or a building within the complex that was more remote and more fortified than the rest.

But he was handicapped by the fact that nobody in Fox Hound Command knew what Metal Gear looked like. Was it something so big it needed a huge protected structure to house it? Or so small that it was only a deadly microchip, computer-triggered or radio-controlled? A barbed-wire fence around a building was no guarantee that Metal Gear was to be found inside. It could be anywhere in Outer Heaven, even in Colonel Vermon CaTaffy's shirt pocket.

All he had to go on was the name, Metal Gear. Somehow that hinted to Halley that the weapon itself was large and needed a sizable building to itself.

Crossing the field that separated the outside fence from the windowless complex of Outer Heaven, the young Marine captain spotted a door at the base of one of the buildings. Using the key card, Halley placed it in the slot on the door, face down. He could hear the latch click, and he pushed gingerly at the door. It opened to his touch.

He was inside now, on the first level of the first building. He pressed himself against a wall, becoming a shadow, and let his eyes do the walking. There were many doors along the hallways of Building One, and all of them were guarded. Armed and uniformed terrorists, most of them carrying high-tech automatic weapons, were everywhere.

Solid Snake knew that at least at the start he would have to avoid the guards wherever possible. Once he knew his way around, and once he'd located a weapon of his own, he'd be able to fight, For now, though, the only intelligent thing was to remain concealed. But for how long would Halley's concealment be safe or effective?

There had to be surveillance devices everywhere in the compound. Halley scanned the walls and ceilings for the telltale red eye of a video camera, but didn't see one. That could mean the cameras were hidden from view, or it could mean that other types of sensors might be operating.

Heat seekers or motion detectors, for example. They were common devices, frequently used in securing premises. Those would certainly tip off the terrorist leader to the presence of an intruder.

But if that were so, wouldn't the patrolling guards confuse the sensors? No, it had to be hidden video cameras, linked to some giant console control board somewhere in the complex.

Solid Snake looked around for stairs leading to the upper floors, but he didn't see any.

Two elevators—east and west, according to Halley's compass—were all that were available to Solid Snake to get him from the first level to another floor. The elevators were an added risk and posed a real danger of possible entrapment. Also risky were the corridors leading to the elevators; there were three of them.

Halley took the one to the left. He found himself facing three doors.

He tried his key card on the first door, but it didn't respond. Why not? The slot for the card was there. Why didn't the door open? Unless . . .

For the first time, Solid Snake realized that there might be more than one key card. In fact, now he was certain of it. Each individual card opened only a small designated number of doors, and it would take more than one to open all the doors.

How many Keys would Justin Halley need to fully penetrate Outer Heaven? Although Justin didn't know it, there were actually eight key cards that, used together, unlocked all the doors in the compound.

It was an elaborate system in which the higher the soldier's rank, the more key cards he was entitled to carry. Only Colonel Vermon CaTaffy himself carried all eight key cards; his two most trusted terrorist aides were entitled to six each.

But the key card in Solid Snake's possession did manage to trip the second lock and get the second door open. Halley slipped inside the room.

It was a small room, little more than a closet, and it smelled bad, like chemicals. The room gave the young Marine a bad feeling, and he wanted out of there. But first, he forced himself to look around.

Something was lying on a shelf near the door. Halley grabbed it and ducked back outside. The door clicked shut behind him, locked again.

He looked at the thing he was hold

in his hand. It was a gas mask. Considering the chemical smells, the gas mask made perfect sense. It was probably used during experimentation in that room.

It could be useful, but what Solid Snake really wanted was a weapon. But he decided to keep the gas mask and moved down the corridor.

The guards were still patrolling, back and forth, up and down. Now they were coming Halley's way. Their heavy boots, making cadenced footsteps, sounded closer and closer. Hugging the wall, Halley raced off in the opposite direction, to the nearest side door of Level One.

Quickly, he tried his key card, which he now thought of as Key Card One. It worked, the door opened, and Halley was back outside the building before the terrorist guards caught a glimpse of him.

Three military trucks were parked just outside the door. They were marked with the same strange insignia of the other vehicles he'd seen outside the compound. Halley ran swiftly toward them, hoping to find them unguarded. He was lucky. No terrorists guards were in sight.

Quickly but thoroughly, Justin began to search the trucks. He was looking for something — anything — that could be useful in his mission.

Luck was with him. In the left-hand truck, his fingers closed around a familiar something — a pistol grip. Justin Halley had to bite his tongue to keep from letting out a yell of triumph.

But his moment of triumph was brief. Halley had found a handgun — the Baretta M92F — a lightweight weapon, yet accurate and deadly. But with it there was no clip of ammunition; the gun was empty.

Still, it was a beginning.

GAME HINT

Get the rocket launcher on the second floor of Building Two. After you have earned four stars, call JENNIFER on frequency 12048.

CHAPTER SIX

Freeing the Prisoners

Quickly, Solid Snake pocketed the empty Baretta and moved on to the right-hand truck. He avoided going near the truck that was parked in the middle, convinced that it was a trap. He'd noticed a thin, almost invisible wire snaking from under the truck's chassis, and rightly presumed there was a detonator somewhere and explosives in the truck.

But maybe the truck on the right had some clips of ammo stashed in it to use with the gun. He searched it carefully, but it yielded up nothing in the way of bullets. It did have a special steel pocket hidden in the door of the cab. Using all his strength, Halley forced it open, and found some antitank mines. Good. These might come in handy. Halley added the mines to the small but growing arsenal he was beginning to put together.

With the mines and the Baretta, Halley made his way back across the compound, and used his key card to get back inside Building One.

Peering around a corner, Halley could see the guards approaching. He was close to the east elevator; it was his only chance. He dashed quickly to it, and used his key card to get the door open. The guards passed an instant after the elevator door closed. They saw nothing.

Halley pressed the elevator button for the third floor. He'd decided to try to proceed systematically from the top floor down. But when the door opened, Solid Snake caught a glimpse of something familiar. Little red eyes.

There were infrared sensor cameras on the third floor. Unblinking, all-seeing little red eyes. The young Marine captain had to keep tight up against the walls to avoid the surveillance lenses. He figured that the entire complex must be monitored — some parts with cameras, others with heat-sensing or motion-sensing devices. How long would he be able to escape detection?

Justin Halley suspected that the evil Colonel CaTaffy was using part of Building One as prison cells for the Snake Men he'd already captured. It was part of Halley's mission to set them free, but Commander South had warned Solid Snake that perhaps some of the Snake Men had turned double agent, and shouldn't be trusted.

Halley found that hard to believe. The men in his squad had all been courageous, highly trained, loyal, and patriotic. The Snake Men were the best, hand-picked. Their special forces training was the toughest in the world. Only the handful that came out of it in one piece were allowed to call themselves Snake Men. How could they change? What kind of torture could even a fiend like Colonel CaTaffy devise that would make a Snake Man betray his commander, his squad, and his country?

Because Solid Snake still had only one key card, he could only go in through the doors it opened. The first few doors he tried failed to respond to the card. But the fourth door opened when the key card was inserted. In the center of the room, a prisoner was tied in a chair, moaning, nearly unconscious.

The prisoner was Chuck Robinson, a Snake Man, a good friend.

Halley should have stopped in the doorway to assess the situation for potentially lethal booby traps or explosives. All his training had prepared him for caution above everything.

But he couldn't help it. When he saw Chuck in that chair, he ran forward to his buddy's side.

"Chuck! Chuck! It's me, Halley!"

The man stirred and raised his head

a little. "Solid Snake? Justin, is that you?"

"It's me, good buddy. Let me get these ropes off you. Think you can stand up?"

"I ... I'll give it a try."

But Robinson was not in any shape to stand. When the ropes came off, he fell to the floor in a heap.

"It's no good, Halley. Leave me here. Try to set some of the others free; they may be able to help you. Maybe if I rest awhile ... "

Solid Snake was reluctant to go, but there were over a dozen other prisoners — if they were alive. He had to find them and set them free. They were his Snake Men brothers, his comrades-in-arms. He couldn't leave them here to die.

"Listen ... Justin. This is very important. ... The heat panels ... the heat panels ... "

"Don't try to talk, Chuck. Just take it easy."

"No ... no ... you've got ... to listen to me. The heat panels ... you can't get to Metal Gear without ... crossing ... the heat panels ... they're terrible ... terrible ... burning ... they burn."

Chuck's delirious, thought Solid Snake. He needs medical attention badly.

"Eat the rations. Eat the rations

You've got to have plenty of rations . . . if you want to . . . make it through . . . or you'll die on the heat panels."

Chuck kept mumbling the same words, over and over, his voice weak but his words heavy with urgency.

"Right, good buddy. Will do," said Solid Snake softly. "Listen, Chuck, I'm going to leave the door unlocked for you. Try to make it out of here. If you can't, I'll come back and get you after I finish with Metal Gear. Is that a go?"

Chuck nodded wearily. "But the heat panels . . ." he said again. "Listen to me. You've got to raise your own body temperature . . . if you want to survive . . . you gotta eat."

"I hear you, Chuck."

"Take care, Solid Snake."

Halley nodded grimly. "I'll take care," he promised.

The key card opened other doors, in which he found several more Snake Men prisoners. All of them had been tortured, and several of them were unable to speak. It almost broke Justin Halley's heart to see his friends in such a condition. He set the men free, promising to return and get them all out to safety, once his mission was completed.

So far, none of the rooms had contained any ammunition for his Baretta. He needed weapons to penetrate the inner defenses of Outer Heaven. He had to keep looking.

From one of the rooms on Level Three, Solid Snake could sense something seeping from under the door. The odor, bitter and stinging, was unmistakable to anyone with Halley's training. Poison gas.

Halley put on the gas mask. Should he avoid this room or go into it? His sense of survival told him to stay clear of the poison gas. But his logic told him something different. Why would the terrorists bother to gas the room unless they had something of vital importance hidden there?

Solid Snake had to take the risk. Using his key card, he got the door open.

It was a large room, and at first it appeared to be empty. But as Solid Snake crossed it, wearing his gas mask, the floor suddenly tilted up, sending him lurching backward, barely able to keep his balance. There was a terrible rumbling sound, growing louder and louder. Through the fog of poison gas that filled the room, Solid Snake found it difficult to make out what was happening.

Then he saw it. The deadly trap.

A huge rolling device, a giant steel pin,

eight feet long and weighing three thousand pounds, heavy enough to crush a man to death, detached itself from the wall and came rolling across the sloped floor, coming at him at top speed. Unless it was stopped, in only a few seconds it would smash the life out of Solid Snake.

GAME HINT

Avoid surveillance cameras by staying next to the walls.

CHAPTER SEVEN

A Terrorist's Face

The deadly roller came thundering closer. The floor tilted crazily. Solid Snake staggered and found it impossible to stay on his feet. The pin was moving more rapidly, gaining momentum with every second that passed. It was moving a lot faster than Halley, and soon it would be on top of him. Solid Snake thought fast.

Crouching down to the floor, Halley waited and watched as the pin got closer. At the precise moment that it reached him, Solid Snake gave a mighty leap upward and threw himself over the pin, rolling clear on the opposite side.

The pin thundered onward, smashing into the far wall. The floor, whose tilt was electronically clued in to the rolling of the steel monster, became level again.

As the floor straightened out, Halley scrambled to his feet, shaky but unhurt. Before he could catch his breath, three terrorist guards came rushing out of concealment, weapons drawn. Solid Snake still had no ammunition for his handgun, and the mines were useless in this situation. All he could do was run. He was near the door, so he raced for it on the double. Without looking back, he pulled it shut behind him, using Key Card One to lock it. The guards were shut inside.

Without delay, Solid Snake used his key card on the next room, and the door swung open. Cautiously, he entered. The room at first appeared to be completely empty — no guards, no lethal devices. In the center of the floor stood only a table, with a computer and some field rations on it.

Were the rations poisoned? Halley hoped not, because he knew he'd have to take the chance anyway. Chuck's words came back to him. *"You've got to have plenty of rations if you want to make it through the heat panels."* Maybe Chuck hadn't been delirious after all.

Solid Snake picked up the rations and sniffed at them. They smelled terrible, but all field rations smelled terrible.

Justin Halley ate some and pocketed the rest. Then he turned his attention to the computer on the table. It sat there, switched off, silently mocking and defying him. What was its purpose? What information did it hold?

Solid Snake reached across the table and turned the computer on.

At once, the screen lit up and showed an enemy terrorist's face. It was the face of Colonel Vermon CaTaffy!

Before Halley had time to think, the face on the computer screen began to decompose right before his eyes. The picture turned into blocks, and the blocks were quickly scrambled until the face was an unrecognizable jumble.

A small clock appeared on the screen, ticking the seconds down from twenty to nineteen . . . to eighteen . . .

Halley realized that this was a crucial identification test. The computer thought he was a terrorist and was putting him through a special run, to make certain of his identity. Each person using this computer screen had only twenty seconds to unscramble the face. The guards were trained in this exercise but Halley was not.

Quickly, Solid Snake began to strike the keys almost at random, while the seconds ticked down one by one.

On the screen, a couple of pieces fell into place, and Halley worked faster, but at the same time with more focus. The trick was to pay as little attention as possible to the clock counting down from twelve to eleven to ten to nine. Just get the job done!

Five ... four ... Halley had only three pieces of face left to go, but one piece he'd unscrambled before was in the wrong place and was blocking the right piece.

Deep breath. Do it, just DO IT! Three ... two ...

The final piece clicked into place a nanosecond before the countdown stopped. There on the screen, the terrorist's face had been reassembled.

Solid Snake heard a click. From a slot in the side of the computer came a small sound, and a key card slid out. His reward for getting it right — a key card. The computer had fallen for his trick.

He compared it to the first key card he had found and noticed that there was a pattern to the bumps on the card. With two cards in hand, it was easy to see that the pattern was a numbering system. This was card two! The bumps were carefully laid out in sections — he could tell that there were eight cards in all.

Now he had more rations and another precious key card.

The next room couldn't be opened with Key Card One, but the door did open at the press of Key Card Two. Inside, was another bound Snake Man prisoner, Jim Tibbett.

"Solid Snake, thank God you're here!

I'd just about given up hope. I have a message for you, from DIANA. She says, 'Grey Fox infiltrated the enemy several days ago. They captured him, but he is alive.' "

Grey Fox was squad leader of the Snake Men. Could Justin Halley rely on the truth of that message? How could DIANA have gotten through to Jim? And when? Before he was captured? Could he trust Tibbett? Or was this only some kind of lying trick to divert Solid Snake from his main objective, Metal Gear? Halley looked deep into Snake Man Jim's eyes, searching for the truth. It seemed to him that he saw it there; but if he were wrong, if Jim Tibbett was lying and Halley believed him, the mistake could easily prove fatal. Yet, he really wanted to believe that Grey Fox was still alive.

What should he decide? Solid Snake was torn between his desire to set his friends free and get them to safety, and his mission — to find Metal Gear, wherever and whatever it was — and destroy it.

It was a hard choice, but the mission came above everything. Those were his orders, and he was here in Outer Heaven to obey them. If on the way he found Grey Fox alive, that would be the icing on the cake, but he couldn't stop to look for him.

Yet, he resolved in his heart to keep

his eyes open for Grey Fox, and to question every prisoner he set free about the squad leader. If anybody could help him on this mission, it was Grey Fox.

"I'll come back for you as soon as I can," Halley promised Tibbett. "Hang in there, Jim. Rest up. The door is unlocked now, so be careful."

"I will," Jim replied, weakly shaking Justin's hand. "You be careful, too."

In the next room, opened by Key Card Two, Halley was hit by odorless poison gas as soon as the door opened. He felt his lungs choking with pain. With only seconds to spare, he got his gas mask on.

Something caught his eye, even through the gas. Taped to the baseboard on the far wall were three clips of ammunition for the Baretta. Bullets. Now he felt like a combat Marine again; now Solid Snake was armed.

In the same room, he found a small package containing the silencer for the Baretta. That made Solid Snake grin, and he screwed the silencer onto the end of the barrel.

The next space he entered was a small armory, a supplementary weapons stash. On a high shelf, Justin Halley located a grenade launcher and a cache of grenades.

This find slowed him down somewhat, but it was too important to leave behind. Solid Snake strapped the grenade launcher on his back, and slung a heavy bandolier of grenades over his chest.

Now he looked like a fighting man.

CHAPTER EIGHT

Captured!

"Hello?" whispered Halley urgently into his compass. "Hello? Control, do you copy?"

Was there anybody on his side listening to him, monitoring his whereabouts? Halley didn't know.

Doggedly, Solid Snake kept moving forward, from one room to another. He hoped to find Grey Fox, but his first priority was to locate a transceiver radio as soon as he could. Time was crunching Justin Halley. He needed to receive his radio messages from Control to guide him further into the depths of Outer Heaven. And he had to have those radio transmissions soon.

Halley was feeling isolated, as though he'd been completely cut off from Fox Hound Command. He didn't even know if his homing device, the compass, was operational. Was the base receiving him? Were they tracking him? Did they even know he was still alive?

Taking the elevator down to the first

floor, Solid Snake made up his mind to try Key Card Two to open those locked doors that hadn't responded to him when he had only Key Card One. To locate Metal Gear, he would need a lot more clues.

Halley emerged from the elevator into a part of the level that was used as a storehouse. It was piled high with evenly stacked rows of heavy wooden crates, each one large enough to house a small truck or an all-terrain vehicle.

Making his way through the stacked-up wooden crates, which were painted with the Outer Heaven insignia, Justin Halley narrowly avoided a deadly trapdoor between two of them. But as he did, a nail protruding from one of the crates caught his sleeve and yanked at his arm.

The compass went flying out of Solid Snake's hand, down into the well of the trapdoor and out of sight.

Solid Snake was stunned. He believed the compass to be his actual homing device, sending out a signal that only Fox Hound Command could receive. He didn't know that the real homing device was sewn into the sleeve of his camouflage suit. Now Justin thought the loss of the compass had cut him off totally from Fox Hound Command!

He'd have to act completely on his

without any thought of backup help from the U.S. Marines or Commander South. But perhaps, when he found the radio, DIANA might be able to guide him.

Solid Snake's search for the radio doubled in intensity. And there were still more Snake Men to set free. Some of them might have important clues for him. Halley moved swiftly, silently, cautiously, from room to room.

In one of the Key Card One rooms, a prisoner named Frank Witkowski gave Justin Halley an important clue:

"Grey Fox is locked up in a hidden solitary cell room. The best way to get to the hidden cell is to let the enemy capture you on purpose."

Let the terrorists capture him! Actually surrender to the enemy in order to infiltrate more deeply! It might be a workable plan. Could this guy Witkowski be lying to trick him? Halley freed the prisoner and, thinking hard, set off again by himself.

Looking through a door, Halley spotted three trucks parked in a row near the outside wall. Solid Snake had been lucky with trucks so far, locating rations, weapons, and necessary equipment in them. Could he get lucky again?

Yes. In one of the trucks was an Ingram Mac II submachine gun with a full clip.

With the Baretta, and now the lightweight, rapid-firing automatic Mac II, not to mention the grenade launcher, the grenades, and the antitank mines, Solid Snake was becoming a walking arsenal, ready for any fight.

But it was also a pretty heavy load for one fighting man to carry. Maybe he'd make better time if he didn't have to walk or run everywhere. For example, if he had wheels. Halley decided to commandeer one of the trucks.

It was at that very moment that Justin Halley's luck ran out.

As he climbed into the cab of the truck, a squad of terrorists appeared as if out of nowhere. Suddenly, Solid Snake was surrounded on all sides. There were guards everywhere, each man with an automatic weapon aimed straight at his chest.

There were no options left; there was nothing to do but surrender. Halley put his hands up and allowed the terrorists to take him quietly.

Captured! Solid Snake was a prisoner! Did this mean that his mission was at an end, a failure? Had he let the Corps down, betrayed the Snake Men squad, Commander South, his country, and the free world?

Halley suddenly recalled the words of Frank Witkowski, the last prisoner freed: *"The best way to get to the hidden cell is to let the enemy capture you on purpose."* Could that Snake Man be right? Solid Snake was about to find out.

Roughly, the guards stripped Halley of his bandolier of grenades, the gas mask, the Baretta, the Mac II, the antitank mines, the ammo, the grenade launcher, the binoculars, the rations. They confiscated all of Solid Snake's weapons and equipment, or at least they thought they did.

But there was one crucial exception. CaTaffy's men missed something.

Because the terrorists could not conceive of Solid Snake having key cards in his possession, because they believed that he'd brought his own weapons into Outer Heaven with him, and because the key cards were no larger or thicker than an American Express card, the guards didn't find them when they frisked him for more weapons.

The key cards were still safe, deep down in the pocket of Solid Snake's camos.

Now that he was a prisoner, what were the odds against his meeting Grey Fox? Witkowski had told him that the terrorists had the squad leader hidden away somewhere in solitary confinement.

The guards spun Justin Halley around, and a black, greasy blindfold was tied tightly around his eyes. He could see nothing. Prodding Solid Snake along painfully with their weapons, they marched him, stumbling, inside a building and down a long corridor. They turned so many corners that Halley couldn't hold onto his sense of orientation. He had no idea where they were taking him.

At last, they reached a stopping point. The terrorists yanked cruelly at Solid Snake's arms to get him to stop. Justin Halley heard a cell door open and he was pushed roughly inside, falling to the hard stone floor. The triumphant and mocking way the guards were laughing and sneering at him told Halley plainly that his interrogation would be next, and very soon. The guards didn't even bother to tie Justin up, another indication that they expected to be back for him within the hour.

The door clanged shut. Reaching behind him, Solid Snake struggled with the thick knot of his blindfold until he got it off. The cell was so dimly lit that it was hard to make out anything except shadows, but in a few seconds Halley's eyes had adjusted to the lack of light, and he looked around him.

There was a chair in the corner, in which was tied a single prisoner, barely conscious. He was bound and gagged.

Justin Halley went to the prisoner. He removed the gag and untied the ropes t¹

were cutting sharply into the man's wrists. Gently, he lifted his head to look at his face. The man's features were so swollen as to be unrecognizable.

"Can you talk?" Justin whispered. "It's me, Halley."

"Solid Snake," the man whispered back through cracked lips. "So they sent you! I'm Grey Fox."

The prisoner's voice faltered, and his words became so faint that Halley had to press his ear against the squad leader's lips to hear what he'd say next.

"Listen . . . carefully. We have very . . . little time. . . . The enemy . . . is constructing the final weapon . . . Metal Gear."

"How close are they to having it finished?" demanded Justin.

"Very close, perhaps . . . less than . . . an hour away." Grey Fox's words came slowly and painfully.

"Hang on, Grey Fox," urged Solid Snake. "Don't leave me now. I need you. Can you describe Metal Gear? How does it work? Is it large . . . small?"

"No. None . . . of . . . the Snake Men . . . has seen it."

"Do you know which building it's in?"

"No. It's . . . very well . . . hidden. You're going to need a map."

A map! What map? This was the first

that Halley had heard about a map to Metal Gear.

"Where will I find this map?" he asked intently.

The squad leader tried to raise his head, but couldn't. "I . . . don't . . . know. I only know there . . . is . . . one."

"What about Doctor Pettovich?" Solid Snake asked. "Have you any clue to where they may be holding him?"

Grey Fox shook his head painfully. "He . . . he . . . could be anywhere. Ca-Taffy . . . keeps moving . . . him around."

"And Ellen, his daughter?"

"Is . . . she . . . here . . . too?"

"Yes, CaTaffy's men kidnapped her in order to make Doctor Pettovich talk."

"Didn't . . . .know . . . that." It was obvious that Grey Fox was fading quickly. He needed a doctor. Halley felt the urgency of the situation tightening around him. This was the leader of his squad. He couldn't just let him die. He had to rescue Grey Fox.

"Solid Snake . . . listen . . . not much time . . . can . . . can . . . you get us . . . out of here before . . . they come back for us?"

"I'll try," promised Halley.

But with what? His bare hands?

CHAPTER NINE

The Escape

Halley's hands were bare of weapons or equipment, and time was running out. The clock of doom was already ticking, ticking. CaTaffy's terrorists would be back for them very soon, and that would mean certain death for the two Snake Men and the total failure of the Outer Heaven mission. What was Halley to do?

His rigorous Snake Man training had taught Solid Snake ways in which he could create whatever he needed from his immediate environment. He looked around him. What was there in this bare cell that he could use? Halley concentrated, visualizing possible escape scenarios.

One piece of luck gave Halley the slightest edge. Along with the two key cards, the terrorists had missed the little book of matches that Justin had found in the truck. Now, if Solid Snake was careful with them, they would at least have some illumination in this dark cell.

And maybe the matches would even

be more useful than just shedding light. Because, although the cell was sealed tightly, Halley thought he could feel the merest whisper of cold air seeping in from outside. Somewhere there must be a crack in the cell wall.

Lighting a match, he held it up as long as he could before it burned his fingers. Yes, there was a thin trickle of cold air coming in from somewhere outside the cell. The flame was flickering only in one direction.

Halley lit up another match, and held this one somewhat lower down, next to the wall. The little match head of fire told him that air was flowing from that direction. With the third match burning, Solid Snake got down on his hands and knees and looked intently. He had to find the air flow before he used the book of matches up completely.

Before the match burned out, Halley's hands found the small gust of air, and his eyes detected the beginnings of a crack in the wall, very close to the floor. He got down on his stomach, as close to the wall as he could, and inspected, feeling the wall carefully with his fingers.

Yes, there was a fault in the masonry. A tiny crack in the wall, just beginning to break through to the other side. Now, if he could only locate the weakest point in the fault . . .

Solid Snake's fingers felt around until they touched the softest part. He felt the masonry beginning to crumble a little under his touch.

Satisfied, Justin Halley sat back on his haunches. "Hold tight, Grey Fox," he said. "Keep it together, and don't go dying on me now. I think maybe I see a way to get us out of here."

Reaching over to where he'd dropped his blindfold when he'd torn it off, Solid Snake picked it up and folded the greasy cloth into three thicknesses. He wrapped the wad tightly around the knuckles of his right hand and made a strong fist. He stood up and squared his shoulders.

Then, taking a deep breath and letting it out again in a tiger's roar, Halley ran toward the wall at top speed. At the last moment, he dropped down and aimed a karate punch with his wrapped fist straight at the center of the crack in the masonry, in the very heart of its weakest spot.

Instantly, the bricks and mortar gave way, and a hole opened in the cell wall. Scratching with his bare hands, Halley enlarged the hole. He had to work fast; the terrorists would be back any moment now.

At last the hole was large enough for a man to pass through. Gently, Justin Halley lifted the weak Grey Fox in his arms as though the big man were a child, and carried him to the hole, pushing him through to the other side of the cell wall. Then Solid Snake squeezed through the hole and stood up, brushing mortar and brick dust off his camos.

Now they were free, but Grey Fox was too weak to stand, and Solid Snake was without a weapon. He would have to stash his squad leader in some relatively safe place, and make an effort to recapture his weapons and other gear, or else find new ones. He'd already lost valuable time — Grey Fox had said he had less than an hour to get to Metal Gear and disarm it.

Because he'd been brought there blindfolded, and because his cell had been so well hidden, Halley had no idea what part of Outer Heaven they were in now. Would either of his key cards work here?

There was a small door behind one of the columns that held up the ceiling, and Halley tried Key Card One on the lock. No go. The lock wouldn't budge.

Key Card Two. He heard a click. All right, this one got the door open. The room was empty — no prisoners, no equipment. It was probable that Grey Fox would be as safe here as anywhere else in the compound.

"I'll be back for you as soon as I can," Halley told his squad leader. "Try to stay alive, Grey Fox. We'll get through this thing."

"You're a good man, Solid Snake," Grey Fox barely whispered. "If anybody can succeed in this mission, it's you."

The squad leader reached inside a pocket. "One last thing," he said. "Take these goggles. They're infrared. There are laser traps on some of the floors. You can see them with these goggles."

Solid Snake left Grey Fox lying on the floor of the room, and closed the door behind him, making a mental note of the layout so that he could find his squad leader later . . . if there was a later.

Without even knowing which level he was on, or in what building, Justin Halley resumed his search of Outer Heaven, still looking for the radio, for a weapon, and for clues to Metal Gear.

CHAPTER TEN

The Shotgunner

The next room Solid Snake entered had nothing in it. It appeared to be just an empty space.

But Justin Halley had a strange feeling about this place. Something was in here; he was sure of it. He did a quick search, but came up with nothing. Even so, all his instincts told him that something of importance should be hidden here. He looked again, this time even more thoroughly, but once again he found nothing. Perhaps his Snake Man instincts were wrong this time.

He was wasting precious minutes. By now the terrorists would have returned to get Solid Snake and Grey Fox. They would have found them missing, and they'd be searching every inch of Outer Heaven. Reluctantly, Halley turned to leave, to look elsewhere. But . . .

There it was! Something really small caught Solid Snake's sharp, trained eye. High up the wall, close to the ceiling, a thin piece of plastic no bigger than a credit card

A brief touch told him that it was Key Card Three. The young Marine captain retrieved it. He now had three out of the eight necessary cards.

Why were the keys just lying about? Halley was sure that it was a sign of the maniac CaTaffy's arrogance — building a fortress and then leaving the keys in plain sight.

With Key Card Three in his pocket, Halley felt a sense of elation. He was on his way again. Locking the door behind him, he looked around to see where he should go next.

One door on the far wall stood out; it was bigger than the others. Big enough to drive a vehicle through. Trucks and tanks, jeeps and other rolling stock were parked all over Outer Heaven, both indoors and out. Could this room be some kind of armory or supply depot?

If it was, it must certainly be guarded. Solid Snake would have to be even more cautious than usual. He crept up silently to the door, and applied Key Card Three to the lock. And heard the click.

In the next room, which was a supply depot, a huge man, whom Halley recognized from his criminal file as "The Shotgunner," was keeping watch over a large cache of weapons, including Solid Snake's own equipment. The terrorists had brought in the weapons to this central armory for storage after they'd captured Justin Halley.

If there was ever one big ugly monster, it was the Shotgunner. He was armed to the teeth, ready to kill, and he loved his work.

Creeping silent as a shadow, staying close to the wall to avoid detection, Solid Snake entered the armory. He saw the giant shape of the Shotgunner looming in the center of the room, watchful, waiting for an intruder so that he could let fly with a deadly rain of bullets.

In the guard's large hands was the most powerful shotgun that Halley had ever seen. One blast from that gun could tear a gaping hole in the wall of a steel building.

All around him, Halley saw piles of weapons — guns and explosives of all kinds. But getting them into his hands would be a noisy business. Before Solid Snake could even shoulder a weapon, the Shotgunner would have heard him and blown him to the moon.

Wait a minute! There, almost under the nose of the Shotgunner, was a pile of gear on the floor. Justin Halley recognized it. It was his own — the Baretta with its silencer, the Ingram Mac II, his bandolier, the gas mask — all of it, even his rations. Now, if he could only get to it . . .

Using the oldest trick in the book, the ventriloquist's skill of throwing his voice in another direction, Solid Snake made a small sound come from the opposite side of the room.

For a split second, the Shotgunner turned his head, only just long enough for Halley to race past him and grab up his weapons cache. Solid Snake hoped that his hands would first fall on the pistol, because the pistol had a silencer. But he didn't have time to pick or choose. And, as luck would have it, the first weapon into his hand was the Mac II.

The Shotgunner heard him and growled in his throat, a deep, animal sound, an enraged threat. He lifted his mighty shotgun and sighted down the barrel at Halley.

There wasn't a second to spare. Solid Snake didn't even have time to reach for the trigger of his gun. Instead, he whirled and swung the Mac II like a baseball bat, letting the Shotgunner have it on the side of the head.

He heard the angry growl become a grunt, saw the Shotgunner topple over from the force of the blow and the mighty gun fall from his big hands.

Solid Snake knew that the noise of the struggle would have the terrorist guards down on him before he could blink an eye. He had to get out of there — and fast!

But as he was running for the back door, loaded down with his gear, he noticed some equipment among the supplies that might prove very useful — a suit of body armor and a bomb blast suit. Grabbing them, Halley ran for his life, out through the back door. He wasn't aware of it yet, but Halley was about to come face to face with a new hazard — the dreaded heat panels.

GAME HINT

Watch out for the pitfall between the wood crates.

CHAPTER ELEVEN

The Heat Panels

Solid Snake looked around him. He was outside the second building of the Outer Heaven complex, in the shadow of a high wall. His weapons were heavy, and he had to get inside and stash them somewhere safe. He'd never find Metal Gear dragging all this heavy equipment around with him.

About twenty yards away, almost against the wall of the building, Solid Snake saw more trucks, three of them. At once, Halley spotted that the middle one was a trap — Solid Snake Man was beginning to be expert in the way the terrorists thought — and he avoided it.

The first truck was empty. But the last truck on the end held a treasure. Sitting in the glove compartment was Key Card Four.

Suddenly, Solid Snake wasn't tired anymore. He was wired, bursting with energy. Grabbing the key card, he ran for the building and entered through a side door.

The layout of Building Two was not unlike that of the first building in the Outer Heaven complex. There were no stairs evident, just two elevators, east and west. No markings on any of the doors. In the corners of the vast first level, painted on the floor, was that same strange insignia.

Minutes were ticking by quickly. Grey Fox had told Halley that Metal Gear was almost completed. Speed was essential, now more than ever.

Solid Snake realized he needed to find a place to stash the arsenal he was carrying. It would just slow him down. But where was a safe hiding place?

He thought about it a minute, and it came to him. The best place to stash equipment is in a room already filled with equipment, a room locked by one of the four key cards Halley already had. If he could only find a place like that, unguarded, a place he could come back to . . .

Halley found an unlocked room filled with food, and stuffed his pockets full of rations. He made certain that he had all four key cards on him and moved silently to a locked door. Key Card Three didn't fit the lock, but Key Card Four got the door open. Very cautiously, on the lookout for traps, he moved inside.

It was exactly the setup Solid Snake

had hoped for. Weapons and gear lined the shelves of the room. The equipment was out-of-date and appeared to be unguarded. It looked like stuff nobody would want or come to check on. Nobody would bother or notice Solid Snake's stash. He could retrieve it as needed.

Halley began to unfasten his bandoliers, but before he could set down any of his gear, he heard noises approaching the door. He moved fast and low toward the back of the storeroom. Just as the front door opened and an armed squad of Colonel CaTaffy's men came in, Solid Snake saw a small back door to one side of him. He slipped through it before the terrorists could catch a glimpse of him.

He was in a place he'd never been before. Ahead of him stretched a large area made up of what appeared to be solar panels, but couldn't be, because there was no sun in the windowless room to heat them. On the other side of the panels was another set of doors, each of them holding the possibility of escape.

To reach the doors Solid Snake would have to cross the panels. Behind him, he could hear the terrorists talking noisily in the storeroom. His only escape route was across the panels.

He could feel the heat rising off them

while he was still four feet away. Three panels were arranged in a set, two smaller panels on the outer edges, and a larger, more intense-looking panel in the center. On the other side of the area, there was a control panel with switches and dials. Obviously, the panels could be turned on or off.

What were these panels? What function did they perform? At a quick guess, without examination, Solid Snake thought that they were made of silicon, a covering for fuel or energy cells, intended to vent the heat created by an enormous energy source elsewhere. From Metal Gear?

Here they were, just as Chuck had warned him. These couldn't be anything but the heat panels.It had been a true warning, after all. Now the Snake Man's words came back to him again: *"You can't get to Metal Gear without crossing the heat panels ... burning ....they burn ....eat the rations. ....You've got to raise your own body temperature ... if you want to survive."*

Rations. Solid Snake must eat — right now. He pulled the rations out of his pockets, and peeled the wrappings off.

Halley swallowed quickly, almost choking on the dry and densely compressed rations, with no liquid to wash them down. He ate as much as he could find in his pockets, then turned to the deadly heat panels.

He couldn't afford another moment's delay. The only way to turn off the heat panels was from the other side of the room. Solid Snake set off across the silicon cells. The heat was fierce, burning...just like Chuck had said.

As Halley crossed the deadly panels, the temperature began to rise even higher. The heat became more intense and more intolerable the further he progressed. And he was still on one of the outer panels. What would happen when he got to the center panel, the one that could really burn the flesh off a man's bones?

Solid Snake had eaten every scrap of field rations he had with him and he still had to face the central panel — without more rations. Suddenly, though, he felt a rise in his own body temperature. The calories he'd eaten were taking effect. His body and internal organs were heating up to match the heat of the panels.

He didn't understand why it worked, but Chuck's advice had saved his life. He was crossing the center panel now. Sweat was running down his head and body. His eyes ached from the heat haze and the glare.

But Solid Snake was still alive. Thanks

to Chuck's warning, the rations had their effect. He was in great pain, but he couldn't bother about that now. Instead, Justin was elated, because he felt he was getting closer to Metal Gear.

Justin Halley stumbled off the heat panels, more dead than alive. The first thing he had to do was shut off the heat. Finding the control board for the heat panels, Solid Snake closed the system down.

Across from him were three doors. He opened the door on the left with Key Card One and stepped through.

GAME HINT

You need the rocket launcher to defeat Arnold.

CHAPTER TWELVE

The Moving Bridge

Laser traps were everywhere, their destructive invisible rays crosscutting and intersecting the hallway about four feet off the ground. Any one of them would have burned a hole right through Solid Snake. Any two of them together would have turned him into Swiss cheese.

Avoiding the laser traps by means of the infrared goggles, Halley made his way to the west elevator. He thought he might be able to spot the location of Metal Gear from the roof.

Solid Snake took the elevator to the rooftop. Two terrorist guards were waiting for him, but Halley threw himself to the floor of the elevator and pressed the button to go down. Bullets penetrated the elevator door, passing over his head.

How to get back safely to the roof? Maybe he could trick the guards. Halley left the elevator at the floor below, and pressed the button to send it back up to the roof. Then he raced for the east elevator.

Halley stepped out of the east elevator

and onto the roof just as the doors to the west elevator were opeing. He watched as the guards let fly with a hail of bullets from their automatic weapons, still believing that Solid Snake was in the west elevator.

But he wasn't. He was behind them, only a foot away from their backs. With the butt of his Baretta he knocked both of them out, cold. They were two more of CaTaffy's men who'd be out of commission for a long time to come.

Ducking down, Solid Snake looked out over the top of the Outer Heaven complex. From the roof, he could see a bridge linking Building One to Building Two, and another linking Building Two to Building Three.

Suddenly, it occurred to Solid Snake that both Dr. Pettovich and Metal Gear might easily be in the third building. With the clock ticking away, perhaps he could reach them without going through any more of the complex. Justin Halley set foot on the bridge.

The instant that Halley took his first steps, the bridge began to move. It was made up of overlapping metal plates and, although it appeared solid, it wasn't.

Under the Marine captain's weight, combined with the weight of his gear, the plates began to shift, one way and the other, making yawning gaps.

This was even more dangerous than the heat panels. Just one small false step, and Solid Snake would fall through a gap to the courtyard below, three long stories down. He'd be squashed like a bug.

Loaded down by a grenade launcher and other heavy equipment, Halley moved with agonizing slowness.

Inch by inch, left foot, right foot . . . He forced himself not to look down, not to think about the concrete pavement three stories below. At last, after long agonizing minutes, Solid Snake crossed the bridge safely. Now he was on the roof of Building Three.

In front of him was a small crate. Halley approached it carefully, then slowly opened the top. He couldn't believe his eyes. There were two objects inside: One was a mine detector, and the other was — the radio transceiver. Now he could hear what Diana was transmitting!

Halley strapped the equipment to his back and walked to one of the elevators. The door wouldn't open. He walked to the other elevator. None of his key cards would open that one either.

So it was back to the rooftop bridge again, for another crossing, to Building Two. But this time he was weighed down by even more equipment. Solid Snake hadn't taken more than three or four steps out into the void when he realized that he was certainly going to fall.

It was better to jump than to fall. It was a long way down, but Halley had made over two hundred parachute jumps. There must be a way to minimize the risk.

With the panels of the bridge swaying and opening under his feet, Solid Snake had to work quickly. First, he put the body armor on. Then he wrapped his weapons as tightly as he could in the bomb blast suit, tying the sleeves around the payload, and paying particular attention to the safety of the radio. Attaching the bandoliers to the bulky package, Halley gently hung them off the bridge and let go.

The weapons landed with a thud. Were they still in one piece? Justin Halley would soon find out. If, that is, he landed in one piece himself.

The bridge was swaying worse than ever, and huge cracks had opened between the plates. With the bridge giving way under his feet, Halley wrapped his arms around his knees, tucked himself into a ball, and jumped over the edge.

Just before he reached the ground, he untucked and gave his body a half twist. As he hit the ground, he rolled over twice, then slapped down hard with both hands.

Scrambling to his feet, Justin Halley

felt himself all over. Nothing broken. He checked his weapons. They seemed to be A-OK. Even the radio didn't have a scratch or a dent on it. Another successful jump, only this time he had made it without the parachute. Not a jump he'd recommend to his squad as a regular exercise. Without his extensive training, he would have broken a leg, or even worse . . .

Solid Snake took a long look around. The courtyard was thick with trucks and tanks. Halley crept into the shadow of a truck for a better look. The truck had rations on the front seat, and he was out of rations, thanks to the heat panels, so he pocketed them.

But there were armed terrorists everywhere. To divert the guards' attention, Solid Snake decided to blow up a tank. Placing a couple of antitank mines under the tank treads, he set the detonators and crept away unseen.

Suddenly, a faint radio transmission, almost blanketed by static, came from his transceiver. What he needed was an antenna, so the broadcasts would come in clearly.

Justin Halley could barely hear a woman's voice saying: "Boss Man here. Watch out! It's a mine field! Try to slip through wearing an enemy uniform!"

The message, coming out of nowhere, left Solid Snake very puzzled. How did Control know where he was? How had they pinpointed him on the edge of a minefield?

Halley had lost his homing device in the trapdoor long ago. But suppose the compass hadn't really been the homing device. The compass had been the only thing that Fox Hound Command had let him take into Outer Heaven.

Except for ...

Except for his suit of camouflage. The camos had come into Outer Heaven on Solid Snake's back. For the first time, Justin Halley realized that somewhere in his suit must be the real homing device. They'd been tracking him all along.

But wait. If Control knew where the mine field was, hadn't it also been aware of the heat panels, the Shotgunner, and every other hazard that Captain Justin Halley had faced?

Why hadn't Control warned him earlier?

Why had his commander lied to him about the compass? Didn't the leader of the Snake Men trust Justin Halley? And now, if Solid Snake were to take off his camos and put on an enemy uniform, wouldn't Halley be off the computers of Fox Hound

Command? And would that be good or bad?

"Can I still trust Commander South?" Halley whispered, and didn't know the answer. He felt totally cut off from his command.

CHAPTER THIRTEEN

The Underwater Tunnel

In spite of the dangers that threatened him, in spite of the suspicions he held, no matter how justified he believed they were, Halley knew that he must continue to follow orders and carry out his mission. His training and discipline would not permit him to disobey a superior officer, even one whose motives were suspect.

If he accepted Control's warning as true and got hold of an enemy uniform, he'd have to keep his camouflage suit with him always, to make certain that the homer was operative. That would add even more weight to the load he was carrying. By now, Solid Snake was carrying with him enough gear for three men.

If he could find the homing device, remove it and take it with him, Halley could leave the suit of camos behind. But first, he had to find an enemy uniform. They didn't come empty. He'd have to empty one.

On feet as quiet as a panther's, Solid Snake sneaked up behind an unsuspecting tank guard and rabbit-punched him. Out cold. Working fast, Solid Snake stripped the guard of his uniform. He slipped out of his clothes and put the body armor on again, this time next to his skin. Then he climbed into the enemy uniform, and made certain the four key cards were safe in his pocket, along with the rations.

Halley picked up his camos and ran his hand carefully over the entire uniform. Sewn into the sleeve, Justin Halley located the miniaturized homing device. Now he wouldn't have to bring along the entire uniform, only the sleeve. Ripping off the sleeve, Solid Snake stuffed it into the pocket of the terrorist uniform he was now wearing.

Employing the mine detector to protect him from hidden mines, Halley took his first steps out on the mine field.

Ba-room! Ba-room! Boommmm! Behind him, Solid Snake heard a series of explosions — the tank he'd mined had been blown sky-high. It was a monumental diversion, noisy and deadly. Frightened terrorists were running in every direction, yelling in fear.

But Solid Snake couldn't stop to look back. Watching every step he took, Captain Halley managed to make his way through the mine field. Just ahead was a storage shed in a clearing. It must hold something vital, thought Halley. Using Key Card Four, he unlocked the shed.

Inside, tied to a chair, was a captured Snake Man. He had been severely beaten. Solid Snake untied the man.

"Bill, it's me" he said. "Never mind the enemy uniform. It's Solid Snake."

The prisoner made gasping noises.

Halley knelt by the wounded man's side, and put his ear close to Solid Snake Man's lips.

"Doctor Pettovich is on the second floor of Building Two," gasped the prisoner, and closed his eyes.

As the man passed out, his fingers pointed to a tile on the floor, one that appeared to be the same as any other tile in the room. But Halley looked more closely.

The tile was loose. He moved it and underneath was Key Card Five. Solid Snake picked it up and pocketed it. Could he believe this man? Was Dr. Pettovich on the second floor? Or was it a trap?

Halley made a thorough search of the storage shed. He picked up more rations and made a very useful find — an antenna. Now the transceiver would work a lot better, and the radio transmissions from Control would come in more clearly.

Justin Halley decided to try for Dr.

Pettovich on the second floor of Building Two, as the dying Snake Man had told him.

But when he reached the second floor, Solid Snake encountered a huge deep tank of liquid between himself and his next objective. Was the liquid plain water or something far more deadly, such as acid? Whatever it was, Captain Halley didn't trust the look of it. Even so, he was going to have to get across it somehow.

He approached it with a probing look, trying to scope it out. In the center of the tank, deep under the surface of the liquid, was what appeared to be an underwater tunnel.

Where did it lead? Was it the entrance to where Solid Snake should go next, or was it another of CaTaffy's traps? Or both?

Once again, Solid Snake was facing a crucial test. The underwater tunnel had to be investigated. But it might be a false tunnel, with no opening at the other end. Captain Halley could be trapped there and drown.

Also, he was loaded down with heavy equipment, weapons he would need to succeed in his mission. Although he was a powerful swimmer, Solid Snake would be hampered by the weight of his gear. And who knew how long the underwater tunnel might be? A few hundred yards? A mile? Ten miles? How long could Halley hold his breath? Which was the fail-safe point, beyond which there was no turning back again? None of these questions had easy answers.

Precious moments were being wasted in "what if's?" There was only one thing to do, and that was to dive in. Strapping his equipment to his back, Solid Snake filled his lungs with all the air they could hold, executed a perfect jackknife into the water and swam toward the underwater tunnel.

Inside the tunnel, it was pitch black. He swam for what seemed to be a very long time. The air in Captain Halley's lungs was depleting fast. But there was still no end to the tunnel. It just went on and on, getting darker and darker. And Solid Snake realized with grim certainty that he was in a trap.

It was already too late to swim back to the starting point. Halley's breath would never hold out that long and he was already beginning to feel lightheaded. He couldn't make it to the surface, because the heavy equipment was holding him down as though he'd been tied to a rock.

The situation appeared to be hopeless.

Solid Snake would drown, and Metal Gear would destroy the civilized world. Yet Halley could not give up. Not while he still had air in his lungs. Suddenly, he saw, at the side of the tunnel, a small door. He swam to it, and tried it. Locked. By now, things were turning black in front of his eyes, and there was almost no air left in his lungs.

Perhaps he could unlock the door with a key card. There was very little time left. He'd have only one chance to get that door open before he blacked out and drowned. Which card should he try? The new one — Key Card Five.

With wet and feeble hands, Justin Halley fished the key card out of his pocket and managed to get it into the lock. He was on the verge of passing out.

And then, the secret entrance opened, and Halley swam through it, into the shallow gutter at the side of the underwater tunnel. As he did, his hand scraped along the side of the tunnel and found something. Without thinking, he held on tightly to what he'd found.

Raising his face to the surface, Solid Snake drew in great, ragged gulps of air. Looking around, he saw that he had reached the other side of the huge tank. He was saved.

Wet and trembling with exhaustion, Solid Snake drew himself out of the pool and lay on the rim, panting and gasping. He'd allow himself no more than sixty seconds to get his strength back, then he had to go on. The mission was waiting; Dr. Pettovich was waiting — maybe even here on the second floor, as the dying Snake Man had said.

Halley scrambled to his feet. As he was about to shoulder his gear, he remembered the something he was holding in his hand, the thing he'd picked up in the underwater tunnel. He looked at it.

It was Key Card Six.

GAME HINT

Don't always believe the map you get or what you hear on the radio — you'll find a lot of misinformation.

CHAPTER FOURTEEN

The Trained Killer Scorpions

The first room Solid Snake opened on the second floor held a prisoner, but it was not Dr. Pettovich, it was a member of the squad. As he released the Snake Man, Halley received this message:

"Listen to resistance fighter JENNIFER on waveband 12048." 12048? According to Commander South's instructions, Justin Halley's transceiver had been set on 12033. Now he reset the wavelength and attached the antenna. Almost at once, Solid Snake heard, loud and clear, a woman's voice coming over the transceiver. It wasn't a voice that he'd heard before. It was not DIANA.

"JENNIFER here. I'll set up the rocket launchers. Come and get one! Over!"

Without delay, Halley went in search of the rocket launchers, following JENNIFER's radio signal by rotating the antenna and using it as a direction finder.

The radio transmission led him around corners and through a long corridor. At the end of the corridor was a row of giant packing crates. Solid Snake realized that the crates might hold the rocket launchers, but most likely were another of CaTaffy's fiendish traps.

Which of them contained the rocket launchers? Which was the trap?

Up to now, Halley had always stayed away from the middle of everything he'd encountered in Outer Heaven — the middle crate, the middle truck. But now he had a feeling. Instinct told him that at this stage of the game Colonel CaTaffy would be ringing in some changes. He thought for the first time the middle crate would be the safe one.

And it was. One more time, Solid Snake's instincts had served him well. The middle crate held the rocket launcher.

Behind the crates, he saw a door, partially hidden hidden behind one of the pillars that held up the ceiling. Using Key Card Six, Halley got the door open. Inside was Dr. Pettovich.

At last! Solid Snake took an eager step forward, then stopped. All of his highly-developed Snake Man instincts told him that something was wrong here. He smelled a trap. Where were the guards? There ought to be guards inside the room with a prisoner as vitally important to the Metal Gear project as Dr. Pettovich.

Taking one of the mines from his arsenal, Halley rolled it gently across the floor to where the "doctor" was sitting tied to a chair. The man didn't move, not so much as the flicker of an eyelash. This isn't the scientist, Solid Snake said to himself, it's a dummy.

A booby-trapped dummy.

Solid Snake fired a burst from his Mac II, and the thing exploded, shattering into wires and stuffing. Halley hurled himself to the floor and covered his head the same instant that the mine under the dummy's chair went off with an ear-shattering blast.

As he picked himself up, and brushed the fragments from his uniform, Justin Halley discovered, in the debris on the floor, Key Card Seven.

The radio began to beep at him, as Control's signal was received again. Halley heard the same female voice. "JENNIFER here. I have a compass for you. Follow my signal. Over."

A thin, high signal began to emanate from the transceiver, and a second or two later it was matched by a transmission coming from one of the locked rooms in the hallway. Using Key Card Four, Solid Snake located the compass. The room next door was unlocked by Key Card Six. It held no prisoners, nothing but a small bottle. Cautiously, Halley opened it, held it away from his nose, and with his other hand fanned a little of the fumes toward his face and took a sniff. Solid Snake recognized the odor of the chemical from his training with the Snake Men. It was an all-purpose antidote to a number of deadly poisons. Quickly, he tucked the little bottle into his uniform belt.

Suddenly, Justin Halley heard the heavy thumping of running boots. Terrorist guards were on the way. He had to get out of there. He raced down a corridor, through a back door and down a set of stairs that took him directly into a desert.

A desert, here in the jungle? Impossible, at least in nature. No, it had to be man-made, another trap of CaTaffy's. Heaven only knew what awaited Solid Snake in the sands of a terrorist's phoney desert.

Oddly, Halley felt elated. The presence of the unlikely desert, here in the middle of nowhere, led him to believe that he was much closer to Metal Gear than before. The more difficult the obstacle, the nearer to the goal.

As Justin Halley took out his compass to lead him across the desert, he heard a strange, whirring noise. It sounded like something shuffling across the hot sands, something huge and dangerous.

Before he could react to the sound, three giant creatures slowly came into view. Halley was nervous. These were trained killer scorpions! CaTaffy used them to destroy his enemies. And now they were coming at him, poisonous stings held high in the sting position. What a horrifying sight! Even a man with the courage of Marine Captain Justin Halley had to turn pale.

The trained killer scorpions were mutants, raised to grow to between fifteen and seventeen feet high. Their poison stings were as long and thick as a javelin. They had eyes that bugged out of their heads on stalks, and the stalks kept twisting this way and that, searching for their quarry.

And they'd caught sight of Solid Snake. He could tell because a horrifying, high-pitched buzzing came out of the three of them, the sound of evil excitement. Slowly, they turned in his direction and slowly they moved toward Halley. Their bodies were covered with scales, and the scales made a sickening noise as they dragged across the burning sands of the desert.

The curled tails of the trained killer scorpions were raised high, poised to strike, to sting, and to kill.

They were slow, but what was the need

for haste? Where could Solid Snake go? The desert, seemingly stretching around him for miles, was empty of shelter, and the sun was hot enough to broil a man alive. He had nowhere to run, nowhere to hide.

But the scorpions loved the desert heat; they thrived in it and grew to enormous sizes. All they needed to survive was furnace heat and the frequent opportunity to make a kill.

Justin Halley would have to stand and fight. He sorted through his weapons as the trained killer scorpions came closer. He could smell them now. They smelled foul. Solid Snake fired again and again, until the clip of his Baretta was empty. And still they came, dragging their scales over the burning sands. Nothing seemed to stop them, not Halley's grenades, nor his Mac II.

He braced himself, dropping a rocket down the breech of his rocket launcher, and aiming through the sight. Solid Snake slammed his hand on the trigger button, and the rocket exploded from the tube. One scorpion exploded in a noxious burst of matter.

He fired again. The rocket launcher was hot to the touch; the disposable firing tube wouldn't take much more use. A miss. Another rocket launched, then another, and the second of the trained killer scorpions blew apart messily. But the third one kept coming at Halley. Nothing appeared to faze the creature, not even the sudden explosive death of its brothers. Its stinger waved over its head, eager to plunge into Solid Snake's heart.

Loading the rocket launcher, Halley hit the trigger button, but it misfired, and the rocket wasn't launched. Was the rocket launcher still operational?

There seemed to be no stopping this evil creature. Ammunition of any kind showed no effect on it. The scorpion would have to be hit head on, with everyting he had.

Solid Snake waited until the monster was almost on top of him. He waited until he could see the color of the creature's beady eyeball. It was green. Then and only then did he turn and aim the rocket launcher dead on target. But would the launcher fire or misfire again?

Ba-room!

The last explosion caught the giant lumbering creature full in the chest. With an eerie high scream, it blew into a million poisonous fragments.

Solid Snake was clear.

CHAPTER FIFTEEN

Ellen

Halley headed across the desert for Building Three of Outer Heaven, determined to let nothing stand in his way. He had to rescue Dr. Pettovich and his daughter and destroy Metal Gear before the evil weapon could be put into use against the nations of democracy. No more Mr. Nice Guy. CaTaffy was asking for it now.

There were trucks parked in front of the building's side entrance, but a few mines took them out. Within seconds, he was in the building and using Key Card Seven to get the elevator working.

On the second floor, the rooms were opened by Key Card Five. Solid Snake let himself into one of the rooms and saw nothing. The room appeared to be entirely empty. And yet . . . Halley felt a prickle along his skin. His trained instincts were telling him that something was here, something of vital importance. He went to the far wall and ran his fingers along the rough stone.

It felt solid, looked solid. And yet . . .

The tips of Solid Snake's fingers touched a line, running like a crack in the stone from the ceiling to the floor. He pressed hard, harder.

The crack widened, and a secret compartment in the wall opened up. A figure was stuffed into the secret compartment, which was barely large enough to hold it. It was a girl, bound and gagged, and unconscious.

Solid Snake took the choking gag off, and revived the girl gently. But when she saw the terrorist uniform that Halley was wearing, she began to scream. The poor girl was obviously terrified.

"*Shhhh*, it's all right," and Halley put his hand firmly back over her mouth. "I'm not one of CaTaffy's men, I'm Captain Halley of the Snake Men squad. I'll take my hand away if you promise not to scream. Okay?"

The girl nodded and mumbled something. Carefully, Solid Snake took his hand away.

"Are you all right?" he asked her in a low voice.

The girl nodded through her tears. "I'm okay," she whispered back.

"Are you Ellen, Doctor Pettovich's daughter?"

"Yes, I am. Have you found my father?" the girl cried eagerly.

"Not yet, but soon, I promise. Both of you will go home safely."

Solid Snake looked at her face carefully. She looked tired and probably hungry, but she didn't seem to have been hurt.

"Look, I'm going to untie you now and take you somewhere to hide. I think you'll be safe until I come back for you. Try to hang in there and be brave."

"I'll try, but I'm worried about my father," said the girl urgently.

"Not as worried as I am," said Solid Snake to himself.

"I'm going to get word to him that you're alive, so don't worry anymore. Stay as quiet as you can and leave everything to me. I'll see to it that both of you get out of here safe and sound. Now, put your arm around my neck and lean on me. You're a brave girl, Ellen. I'm taking you out of here."

Halley left the girl in another room, making a mental note of which door she was behind, then he set off down the corridor. He was convinced that both Dr. Pettovich and Metal Gear were somewhere here in Building Three. Was there a basement in this building? He should check that out without delay.

Neither the east nor the west elevator had a button for the basement, but that meant there could be stairs hidden somewhere. If only he could find them. Maybe he could get some advice from Control. He spun the tuning dial on the radio.

"Solid Snake? Solid Snake? Boss Man here."

It was DIANA, transmitting on the frequency assigned to her by Commander South.

Justin heard the faint radio signal, and he recognized DIANA's voice. But he paid no attention to the transmission. Halley realized now that DIANA's signals had been misleading him all along, and that JENNIFER was really his Control, a true freedom fighter.

The only thing Solid Snake didn't know was how much damage DIANA might already have done.

GAME HINT

Be sure to knock out all the guards *before* you enter the heat panels. Eat your rations midway through.

CHAPTER SIXTEEN

The Map

Solid Snake found himself facing three doors. At first, he decided on the left-hand room, but as he approached it, all his instincts triggered a warning: Don't go in there! He changed his mind for the right-hand door instead, and Key Card Seven opened it.

Halley expected to find a small room, but instead the door opened onto a vast well-lit area, with locked doors running along the sides of the four walls.

Suddenly, from his transceiver came JENNIFER's voicc.

"Be careful not to kill him. He's my brother. If anything happens to my brother, I can't help you anymore."

Her brother? JENNIFER had a brother here in Outer Heaven? But why was she mentioning it now? The room seemed empty.

Halley turned to the first locked door on his left. Using Key Card Seven, Solid Snake opened the door. Three Snake Men prisoners were inside, in a tiny room. The man in the middle was sitting bound, but not gagged.

That man was Bob O'Reilly, Eagle Man, Justin Halley's best friend in the Snake Men squad. When he saw his friend, Solid Snake broke into a wide grin and started toward him, but Eagle Man cried out to him in an agonized voice.

"NO! Solid Snake! Don't take another step toward me. I've been booby-trapped, rigged up to plastic explosives. I don't know where the detonator is. We'll all be blown sky-high if you lay a finger on me. Listen to me, Justin. I am JENNIFER's brother. My life is not important, only the destruction of Metal Gear is important. You're very close now. How many key cards do you have?"

"Seven," answered Halley.

"Good. There are eight key cards, so you need only one more. Metal Gear is hidden in the basement of this building, and Doctor Pettovich is a prisoner there. It's very near to completion, and when it's complete, it will detonate a series of catastrophic explosions all over the free world. You must get hold of Key Card Eight. It's the only card that will unlock the basement location. Every second is precious. Go. Go now!"

"Bob, I can't leave you here like this," Solid Snake protested.

"You don't have a choice, Justin," replied Eagle Man softly. "You'd better hurry."

There was nothing for Solid Snake to do but obey, to leave JENNIFER's brother, his best friend, tied up and booby trapped. Justin left the room. But he didn't get far.

The vital minutes were counting down, but Halley could not leave Eagle Man and the other two Snake Men to die. It was an impossible decision for him to make. He turned back.

As Halley came back into the room, he realized that already CaTaffy's evil was at work. He smelled poison gas. The Snake Men were going to die.

Putting his gas mask on, Solid Snake ran into the room and freed the two Snake Men on either side of Eagle Man, dragging them out. They were barely breathing, but still alive.

Now for Eagle Man. But how to get him out of the poison gas when he was booby-trapped with explosives? In the doorway, Solid Snake watched in horror as JENNIFER's brother's eyes shut and his head fell forward on his chest. The poison gas was beginning to work.

The weight of Eagle Man's sagging body pulled his chair over with him. Instinctively, Captain Halley braced himself against the imminent explosion of the booby trap.

But there was no explosion. As Eagle Man had slumped forward, his fall had pulled a wire loose from the trap. The chair had disconnected the detonator.

Instantly, Solid Snake seized Eagle Man and half-dragged, half-carried his friend out of the gas-filled room. He tried CPR, breathing fresh air down into Eagle Man's lungs, but his friend didn't respond. It looked as though Solid Snake Man were dead.

But Halley wouldn't give up hope. Remembering the little bottle of antidote, he poured some of the liquid down his friend's throat and, in less than a minute, he heard the choking and gagging that told him that Eagle Man was alive.

In jubilation, Solid Snake pounded JENNIFER's brother happily on the back. And then he made a discovery.

Pinned to the back of Eagle Man's uniform, in a mocking gesture of Colonel CaTaffy's, was Key Card Eight, the last card, the one that CaTaffy had never expected anybody to find. He had thought it would be destroyed when the booby trap exploded.

Halley now had the final key card to Metal Gear.

Although he held all eight key cards

and the clue from Eagle Man that Metal Gear was in the basement, Halley still didn't know exactly where to find Metal Gear. He only knew that the basement would be the most heavily guarded place in all of Outer Heaven.

And first, he would have to find the stairs that led to the basement. None of the elevators were programmed to go there. If only he had more time! Justin Halley was slowed down by the equipment he was carrying, but he was afraid to leave any of it behind. Not knowing what he'd be up against, he didn't know which weapons would be most effective.

Did he really need all eight of his key cards? Eagle Man said that the eighth one was the key to Metal Gear. Maybe he ought to think of leaving the other seven behind, so that he wouldn't have to waste even a moment looking for Key Card Eight.

Looking to separate Key Card Eight out from the rest, Solid Snake shuffled through the key cards in his hand, and as he did so, he noticed something for the first time, something most unusual.

On the backs of the key cards were printed different pieces of the same design, like a puzzle. It actually *was* a puzzle, and when Halley had laid the cards out together in a certain way, he saw the design for the first time. It was the same insignia that was all over the compound, painted on the sides of the trucks, the badge on the enemy uniform that Solid Snake himself was wearing — a grinning, fanged reptile entwined around a twisted, broken tree.

The insignia in itself didn't surprise Justin Halley. But there was something more. With the cards all laid out, he noticed for the first time that the design actually incorporated a map of Outer Heaven. There, in the coils of Solid Snake, were the different buildings and levels he'd gone through. He could make out the heat panels and the underwater tunnel and the desert with the trained killer scorpions.

And there, in the center of Solid Snake's eye, was a very small star. Solid Snake knew at once that the star represented the weapon, Metal Gear. The rest of the map showed him exactly where in the basement to find it, and where the stairs must be leading to the basement. Committing the map to memory, Halley went in search of the stairway.

According to the map, the stairway ought to be very near one of the pillars that held up the ceiling of the first level. Swiftly, Halley made his way to the pillar, but saw nothing. No sign of any stairway around it, yet Solid Snake was certain that he was in the right place.

A sudden burst of gunfire chattered angrily past his head. Captain Halley dove for cover. There wasn't any cover, only the presence of the pillar, which he hugged with his body. It wasn't much protection, but it was all there was.

The situation looked hopeless. He was right there out in the open, in the middle of a firefight, and he couldn't even see the terrorists. They were protected, shooting at him from their hiding places. All he could do was stay close to the pillar.

What?

Solid Snake touched something. It felt like a lock, down low in the base of the pillar. A lock! That was it! The stairway wasn't *near* the pillar, it was *inside* the pillar!

Key Card Eight. He had only seconds to find it. Why hadn't he thrown the other key cards away? At last, Key Card Eight was in Halley's hand.

Fitting it into the slot, Halley looked up to see four guards breaking cover, racing at him with assault rifles. There wasn't a second to spare. Would Key Card Eight do the trick?

A click; the side of the pillar opened like a narrow door. Solid Snake, grabbing up his gear, threw himself headlong into the opening and slammed the door behind him.

He found himself falling into total darkness.

CHAPTER SEVENTEEN

Metal Gear

Headfirst, Halley rolled down and down, unable to stop himself. When he finally came to a halt, his head slammed painfully against a step.

Sitting up, Solid Snake felt himself all over to see if anything was broken. Everything hurt, but everything seemed to be intact, although he had a headache that a Himalayan mountain of aspirin couldn't cure.

Just as Halley had hoped, the pillar was hiding a stairway leading to the basement. Of course, he'd expected to be going down the stairs on his feet, not his head. A huge bump was beginning to rise on the back of his skull, but he didn't have the time to pay it any mind.

Hugging the shadows, Solid Snake made his way cautiously down the remaining stairs. He was so close to his objective now that he could almost taste it, but, all of a sudden, he felt his body sagging. Weariness and fatigue overcame him, and he was so tired he could barely take another step.

It was a long, long time since Halley had rested or eaten, and he was out of rations. Also, the weight of the heavy equipment he was carrying was sapping his strength, and his headache, perhaps from a slight concussion, was pounding away inside his skull, making it hard to think straight. He tried to pull himself together, but it was very hard.

Although the young Marine Captain was well aware of the urgency for haste, he was afraid of making mistakes in judgment, given his weakened condition. This was the most crucial part of the mission, and Justin Halley couldn't afford to make one false move.

As Solid Snake entered the basement, he heard guards all around him. Halley knew that they were getting ready to unleash an attack on the free world, putting into operation the most powerful and deadly weapon ever devised by the mind of an evil man.

If he used his weapons here, Solid Snake would reveal his presence before he even got to Metal Gear. He had to act as covertly as he could, disabling guards from behind rather than shooting them. His

Snake Men training — not his powerful guns, mines, or grenades — was the only tactic he could rely on to get him to Metal Gear.

One by one, using nothing but his bare hands, Captain Halley took on the terrorist guards. His expertise in *t'ai chi*, the special breathing and the natural movements of the animal world, made Solid Snake a graceful shadow silently stalking the enemy stronghold.

Like a jungle cat, Halley prowled unseen, and pounced without warning. His karate blows and rabbit punches, delivered with trained precision, took out one enemy guard after another, and all in silence. The odd thing was, that with every terrorist down, Solid Snake felt his strength beginning to return. He knew that he was coming closer and closer to his objective.

And then, turning a corner with the image of the key card map fixed in his memory, Solid Snake came face to face, for the first time, with Metal Gear.

As soon as he saw it, Halley recognized it. Nothing that huge and ugly could be anything else than Metal Gear. It was a tall, wide machine made out of a shining black metal that Solid Snake had never seen before. The metal itself seemed to radiate evil. Could this mysterious unknown metal be the source of Metal Gear's deadly power?

Metal Gear was truly awesome, menacing, and strange. On its side was painted the deadly insignia that Halley had first seen in the jungle and later encountered everywhere in Outer Heaven. But displayed on the weapon the evil markings took on a new and even darker meaning.

Part of the machine was outfitted with a keyboard and a printer, so Solid Snake knew at once that what he'd suspected about Metal Gear was true. It was computer-controlled, and probably hooked up to a network of computers located throughout the terrorist nations.

Even now, the printer was chattering away, issuing a readout target of every major city in the free world. Justin Halley could see two buttons on the control panel, one red and one white, and a digital timer. Standing by the weapon's side, leaning over the instrument panel, were two men. One of them, wearing an elaborate uniform complete with medals and decorations, was none other than Colonel Vermon CaTaffy, the world's leading terrorist murderer. The other man, hunched and broken, was Dr. Ivan Pettovich.

Solid Snake slipped back further into

the shadows to survey the weapon. Metal Gear was housed in an octagonal booth of shatterproof, see-through Lexan plastic. Each of the eight sides was locked, and guarded by an armed terrorist of matchless ferocity, strength and cunning. These were CaTaffy's picked elite guards, his most murderous men.

From the shadows, Halley watched in horror as CaTaffy selected his primary target. Through the Lexan shield, he couldn't hear their voices but the gloating look on CaTaffy's ugly face was hard to miss, and Halley could almost hear that vicious laughter.

Then CaTaffy took a step away from the control panel and Solid Snake could make out on the screen that the chosen target was Washington, D.C.

"No!" The protest was yelled out in Justin Halley's own mind, but from his lips came no sound at all. It was his Snake Men training that kept him silent.

CaTaffy adjusted his coordinates and pressed the red button. The digital countdown in seconds began. The destruction of the free world had begun.

Halley saw the countdown start: 60 ... 59 ... 58 ...

Less than sixty seconds to detonation. In under a minute, Washington would be reduced to rubble. And the other capitals would follow... Ottawa, London, Tokyo, Canberra, Paris, Wellington...

Solid Snake thought faster than he'd ever thought in his life. It was now or never; this was what he'd been sent here to do.

Eight guards. That was less than ten seconds per guard. If Captain Halley attempted to use his grenade launcher or his rocket launcher or his mines, chances were that he'd blow the entire basement sky-high, and it would be too late to disarm Metal Gear.

What would happen to the weapon's nuclear payload that was no doubt hidden somewhere, ready to launch? An explosion could trigger that launch.

Solid Snake dropped all his equipment. Perhaps his body armor would give him some protection.

He glanced over and saw the display: 55...54...53...52...

What about the locks on the Lexan shield? Eight locks, eight key cards. Thank goodness Halley hadn't left the other seven key cards behind. What he had to do now was to defeat each guard in turn, from one to eight, and put the right key card into each lock. When all eight cards were inserted, Solid Snake was sure he'd be able to get to Metal Gear.

It would be mortal hand-to-hand combat, like ancient Roman gladiators, between Halley and each of the terrorist guards in turn. The only advantage on Solid Snake's side was that the guards were unable to leave their posts to gang up on him, because they had to defend their locks every second.

One by one, Solid Snake attacked the terrorists in a struggle for supremacy. The first guard went down. Then the second. More than once, it was only Halley's body armor that saved his life.

From outside, the young Marine heard an incredible racket going on, the indistinct sounds of men's voices yelling, muffled explosions, rapid gunfire.

No doubt the entire terrorist army had been deployed to burst in here at any moment and kill him. Solid Snake was not afraid to die, but he was determined to take CaTaffy and Metal Gear with him.

Each time he overcame a guard, Halley slammed one of the key cards into the slot at one side of the eight-sided shield. One more lock would disengage.

The pressure was building. Halley could see 40 ... 39 ... 38 ... only thirty-eight seconds remaining.

Using all his Snake Man skills, Solid Snake overthrew another guard. But even for the most courageous man in the Snake Men squad, eight killers were too many to defeat in less than a minute. Three were down, but five were still alive, with only half a minute to go. Only three key cards were in their slots. Fewer than half the locks were open.

Perhaps it was the pressure he was under, perhaps it was the pressure combined with his head injury, but Solid Snake suddenly felt as though the battle was all over, and he'd lost. Despair threatened to overcome him, and he felt his energy begin to ebb away.

Halley felt trapped and powerless, as though a strong net had been thrown over his body, and that he was being dragged off to his death, helpless to do anything about it.

It was Justin Halley's worst nightmare, a recurring dream from which he'd wake in a cold sweat. Now it was coming true. He was failing in his mission.

Meanwhile, the seconds kept ticking down toward the destruction of the world.

Suddenly, just behind him, Solid Snake heard the barking of gunfire. The terrorists must have broken through, and the enemy now had him surrounded.

CHAPTER EIGHTEEN

The Final Battle

At the sound of guns firing behind him, Solid Snake whirled around, ready to die, and equally ready to take as many of the enemy with him as he could.

But, to his astonishment, he saw — not the enemy he expected, but JENNIFER's brother Eagle Man, Grey Fox, and other Snake Men he'd rescued, even Chuck. It was his old squad, weak and wounded, but coming to fight at Justin Halley's side. Metal Gear had been their mission, too. Now Solid Snake was no longer alone; now he had allies in the final battle.

Only two of the Snake Men had found weapons. The others began attacking the remaining guards with sticks, pieces of brick and stone, anything they could get their hands on. Weakened though they were by their imprisonment and torture, their united strength caught the guards by surprise, and two more terrorists went down under the Snake Men's assault.

Solid Snake raced over to insert the key

cards in the other two slots. Five guards down. Five locks opened. Three more to go.

Now, Solid Snake needed all the allies he could get. Pushing aside the body of a fallen guard, he shouted through the open lock straight into the Lexan-shielded enclosure.

"Doctor Pettovich! Doctor Pettovich! Ellen is alive! She's safe! We're the United States Marines, and we've rescued your daughter!"

Would the old man hear Halley's words? And if he did, would the words do any good? Dr. Pettovich was already so enfeebled . . . what kind of help could he give?

Inside the Lexan booth, Dr. Pettovich appeared to come to life very suddenly. He stood up straight, and the years fell from his shoulders. Reaching out for CaTaffy's throat, he began struggling with the terrorist leader to get at the white DISARM button.

For a minute there, the combat between the two men was almost equal. But Colonel CaTaffy was a much younger and stronger man, and he was armed. Dr. Pettovich had been subjected to the most vicious physical and mental torture, which had drained him of his strength. Yet, he fought on, made stronger by the knowledge that his daughter was alive.

With an effort, CaTaffy fought himself free of the old man's grip, drew his pistol from its holster, and brutally pistol-whipped the scientist. Dr. Pettovich slumped to the ground unconscious.

But not before proving to Solid Snake what he needed to know. It was the white button the Snake Men had to reach before it was too late. The white button was the only thing that could stop the countdown on Metal Gear.

Time had slowed down, but each second moved too fast. The display read: 24 ... 23 ... 22 ...

The battle continued. Seven of the eight key cards had already opened seven of the locks. Thanks to the help given by the Snake Men, seven of the enemy lay unconscious. But there was still one more guard to go, one more lock to open.

Captain Halley ran towards the guard, uttering his tiger yell at the top of his lungs. The force of his rush knocked the assault rifle out of the guard's hands.

Instantly, the two men were locked in a life-or-death, bare-handed, one-on-one battle. The enemy held the advantage. All he needed to do was to keep Halley away from Metal Gear for a few more seconds, and the terrorists would win. The free world would be destroyed.

The task Solid Snake faced was far more difficult. In the same few seconds, he must overcome the guard, get the lock open, and then defeat the dictator CaTaffy in order to hit that white button.

The enemy guard was fresh and very strong. Justin Halley was almost played out. A man with a mission, for many, many hours he'd been without rest. He'd braved and endured hazard after deadly hazard, fighting for his life every minute. It was a miracle he'd come this far. Did he have enough left to go the rest of the way?

Now a weakened Captain Halley was struggling with the last guard, the strongest of them all. The other Snake Men lay wounded on the ground, too exhausted to help him. But they'd already done their job. Now it was up to Solid Snake alone.

Nothing mattered but that white button.

He could see the countdown continue: 18 . . . 17 . . . 16 . . .

Now the enemy had Solid Snake by the throat, his powerful fingers closing, throttling, trying to squeeze the last breath out of him. Justin Halley couldn't free himself. He was blacking out. Desperately, he looked around for help.

JENNIFER's brother, Eagle Man, was the nearest of the Snake Men. He was lying on the ground, close to unconscious.

"Bob! You have to help me!" croaked Solid Snake, his voice squeezed to a whisper. "Take Key Card Eight from me and put it in the slot. You've got to hurry! Never mind me! Just get the card! We have only a few seconds left!"

Eagle Man raised his head weakly and nodded. Then, painfully, inch by inch, Bob O'Reilly dragged himself over and pulled the card from Solid Snake's fingers. While Halley still struggled with the terrorist, Eagle Man dropped Key Card Eight into its lock. Now all eight key cards were in place.

Things began to happen all at once.

As soon as the last key card fell into place, the Lexan shield dissolved, disappearing into the ground. Metal Gear was now in the open, exposed. But the detonator timer was still ticking the seconds away.

The digital display showed: 15 ... 14 ... 13 ...

The destruction of Metal Gear's Lexan shield took the enemy guard by surprise. For one split second, his hands loosened around the throat of Solid Snake. In that instant, using all his strength and cunning, Halley broke the guard's choke hold.

Now Halley summoned every ounce of strength he had left in his body. With his bare hands, he karate-chopped the last terrorist guard and threw his limp form aside. Without thought for his own safety, Solid Snake hurled himself toward Metal Gear, his right hand reaching for the white button that would disarm the weapon.

But his hand never made it.

As the Marine captain raced into the booth, with only seconds to spare before detonation, Colonel CaTaffy raised his pistol and fired.

The bullet reached its target, slamming into Halley's shoulder above the body armor.

Blood began to pump from the wound. The impact sent Solid Snake's body spinning. But before he reached the ground, he twisted his body in the air like a cat. If he could only...

It was his last possible chance of success, and it worked. Halley fell forward on the computer control panel, his hand outstretched.

He saw the seconds move: 7 ... 6 ...

With an angry roar, the dictator CaTaffy lifted his pistol to fire again. But before he could pull the trigger, Dr. Pettovich, now conscious, reached up from the floor and yanked the terrorist off-balance.

The gun fell from CaTaffy's fingers.

Halley could see he was running out of time: 4 . . . 3 . . . 2 . . .

Solid Snake's hand reached the white button and pushed. The timer clock stopped, the countdown reading 00:00:01. With only one second to spare, Metal Gear was out of commission. The world was safe.

With a beast's snarl of psychotic rage, Colonel Vermon CaTaffy threw himself at Justin Halley. The two men grappled with each other, each trying to get the upper hand.

Solid Snake was younger and stronger than the dictator, but he was wounded and losing blood. CaTaffy was master of every evil dirty trick in the book. The hand-to-hand struggle went on for minutes, and all the while, the noise of a battle taking place nearby became louder and louder, the gunshots sounding nearer and nearer.

Halley reckoned that his fight with Colonel Vermon CaTaffy would be his last. At any moment, the remainder of the terrorist army would be in here, and that would be the end of the Snake Men.

But the mission was a success. Metal Gear was disarmed, and if Solid Snake could only hang on here a little longer, he might be able to take CaTaffy with him. That would really be a blow struck for the free world.

Suddenly, the battle was upon them. A group of armed men in uniforms ran in, brandishing their weapons. At once, Colonel CaTaffy made a dive for the floor, going after his own pistol. Solid Snake saw the action and kicked out with the last remaining bit of strength in his wounded body. The kick caught CaTaffy on the side of his head and knocked him out. The dictator lay sprawled at the side of Metal Gear, the monster he'd created to dominate the world.

"Halley!" cried an astonished voice. "Well, I'll be — Solid Snake, is that you?"

I'm hearing things, thought Justin Halley. It's that bump on the head and the loss of blood. I must be blacking out. I could swear I heard...

"Solid Snake, it's me, Commander South. I'm here with the Fox Hound Command troops and the rest of the Snake Men squad. We've got Outer Heaven completely surrounded. My men are rounding up the last of the terrorists now. I can't believe you're alive. But you're wounded, man. You're bleeding bad. Medic! Get over here on the double. Get this Marine some help!"

"I'm all right, sir, just a little woozy. Take care of my buddies first." Solid Snake pointed to the wounded Snake Men.

"Eagle Man! Grey Fox!" Commander South couldn't hide his astonishment. "Did *you* free them, Halley?"

"Yes, sir. And I found Ellen Pettovich. She's safely hidden. That's Doctor Pettovich, just getting up from the floor. He's on our side, sir."

"And is that . . . thing . . . Metal Gear?" asked Commander South.

"Yes, SIR! Primed, loaded, and out of commission."

"I don't know what to say, Halley, except 'Well done!' Now let's get you out of here and into sick bay. You can tell me all about it when you're feeling better."

"I feel fine, sir, and very glad to see you. But what about CaTaffy, sir?"

"CaTaffy? Colonel Vermon CaTaffy? Was he here?"

"He's out cold, sir, lying right th —"

Solid Snake broke off, mystified. The spot where the dictator had been lying was empty. CaTaffy was not there. "He's gone, sir! He must have escaped! But how — ?"

Halley took one step backward, wobbled, and nearly fell. He'd lost a lot of blood and was getting weaker by the minute.

"Easy now, Solid Snake." Commander South put his arm around Justin Halley's shoulders to steady him. "That evil maniac must have gotten away in the excitement.

He knows every inch of this wretched place. There must be a thousand holes for him to crawl into. Don't worry. One of these days we'll get him. Meanwhile, the chopper is topside, and doctors are waiting."

Halley wouldn't move until he saw the last of his squad buddies loaded onto gurneys. Then, slowly, he followed Commander South out of the basement arsenal.

His job here was done. Solid Snake's mission had been completed, and successfully. Metal Gear was now harmless, and in the possession of the forces of democracy. The Snake Men prisoners were on their way to the best medical attention in the world. Ellen and Dr. Pettovich were safe. The world was safe.

Even so, Halley knew that something was missing. His victory was incomplete, and he had the bitter taste of ashes in his mouth.

In the doorway, Halley turned. He spoke very softly. "Wait for me, CaTaffy," he whispered. "I'll be back, so wait for me. You belong to me, and soon I'll be coming back to collect. Next time you won't get away."

He spoke very softly, but somehow Solid Snake knew in his heart that — hidden away somewhere — Colonel CaTaffy heard his words.

Dear Reader,

I hope you liked reading *Metal Gear*. Here is a list of some other books that I thought you might like:

Across Five Aprils
by Irene Hunt

All Quiet on the Western Front
by Erich Maria Remarque

Call It Courage
by Armstrong Sperry

The Great Escape
by Paul Brickhill

The Survivor
by Robb White

Young Man in Vietnam
by Charles Coe

You can find these books at your local library or bookstore. Ask your teacher or librarian for other books you might enjoy.

Best wishes,

F.X. Nine

MYSTERY THRILLER

Introducing, a new series of hard hitting, action packed thrillers for young adults.

THE SONG OF THE DEAD by Anthony Masters
For the first time in years 'the song of the dead' is heard around the mud flats of Whitstable. But this time is it really the ghostly cries of dead sailors? Or is it something far more sinister? Barney Hampton is sure that something strange is going on – and he's determined to get to the bottom of the mystery . . .

THE FERRYMAN'S SON by Ian Strachan
Rob is convinced that Drewe and Miles are up to no good. Why else would two sleek city whizz-kids want to spend the summer yachting around a sleepy Devonshire village? Where do they go on their frequent night cruises? And why does the lovely Kimberley go with them? Then Kimberley disappears, and Rob finds himself embroiled in a web of deadly intrigue . . .

Further titles to look out for in the Mystery Thriller series:

Treasure of Grey Manor by Terry Deary
The Foggiest by Dave Belbin
Blue Murder by Jay Kelso
Dead Man's Secret by Linda Allen
Fighting Back by Peter Beere